How We Flew That Summer

by

Christina Jenkins

Royal Roots Publishing

An imprint of Royal Roots Creative, LLC
Upper Marlboro, Maryland

Publisher's Note

This is a work of fiction. Names, characters, places, and incidents are the product of the author's imagination. Any resemblance to actual persons, living or dead, events, or locales is coincidental.

For permissions requests, inquiries, or bulk orders, please contact the publisher at:
Royal Roots Publishing
royalrootspublishing@outlook.com
First Edition, 2026

ISBN: 979-8-9943381-3-1
Printed in the United States of America

Cover Design Notice

Cover design by Christina Jenkins.
The cover artwork was created or enhanced using advanced AI technology under a licensed agreement, with full rights and permissions for commercial use granted.

Dedication

For every Black girl who learned to measure risk before joy,
who noticed the ground before she ever trusted the air.

For the girls who were careful not because they lacked courage,
but because they understood consequence early.

For those who carried responsibility in their hands,
who learned how systems work,
and how easily they fail.

This book is for you.
For the strength it took to pay attention.
For the wisdom it took to stop.
For the courage it took to keep going anyway.

How We Flew That Summer

Prologue
The Fall

The rope snapped like the crack of lightning.

It was not a warning sound. It was not slow. It was not something you had time to think about or prepare for. It was sharp and sudden and absolute, the kind of sound that split a moment clean in two. Before it, there was laughter and shouting and a held breath of excitement. After it, there was only chaos.

For one frozen heartbeat, everything stopped.

Mikki's breath caught in her chest, trapped halfway between a cheer and a scream. Toni's hands stayed lifted in the air, phone still aimed upward, the red record light blinking uselessly as if it could not understand what had just happened. Zee was mid-whisper, lips forming the words be careful, the sound never fully leaving her throat.

Then came the scream.

It tore through the trees, raw and ragged, bouncing off bark and leaves like it did not belong to just one person. It sounded too big for one body. Too full of fear. Too sharp to fade quickly.

Jayda was gone.

One second she was there, weight clipped to the pulley, hands tight around the line, braids lifted behind her in the wind. The next, she was ripped from the air, flung sideways and downward like something launched from a broken slingshot. A blur of pink sneakers and brown arms and flying beads flashed between the branches. There was the sickening sound of wood snapping, leaves exploding upward, something heavy hitting something harder.

Then nothing.

Silence rushed in, fast and thick, pressing against Mikki's ears until they rang.

No birds. No breeze. Even the cicadas seemed to pause, as if the whole forest had decided to hold its breath. The only sound left was the faint hum of summer far away and the soft creak of the rope's loose end swaying uselessly above them.

Mikki dropped to her knees at the edge of the platform.

Her clipboard slipped from her hands and clattered against the wood, but she did not notice. Her palms scraped against the rough boards as she leaned forward, eyes wide and unblinking, staring into the space where Jayda had been.

"Jayda?" she said.

The word cracked in the middle, like it could not carry the weight of what it was asking.

"Jayda," she tried again, louder this time. "Say something."

Nothing answered.

Her heart slammed so hard it hurt, each beat echoing in her head. This was wrong. This was not how it was supposed to go. She had measured the angle. She had checked the distance. She had written the numbers down three different times, just to be sure. Numbers did not lie. Plans did not just fall apart like this.

Toni was already moving.

She did not remember deciding to climb down. Her body just reacted, muscles snapping into motion as fear pushed her forward. Her foot slipped on one of the ladder rungs and she barely caught herself, hands shaking so badly she almost missed the next step. Her glasses fogged instantly as tears spilled over, blurring the world into streaks of green and brown.

"Jayda," she whispered, even as her feet hit the ground. The phone was still clutched in her hand, useless now, her recording ruined by the sound of her own breath breaking apart.

Zee did not speak at all.

She moved with purpose, the way she always did when something went wrong. Her heart pounded so hard she could feel it in her throat, but her hands stayed steady as she grabbed the first aid kit they had packed that morning.

Just in case.

She had said it quietly when she zipped it shut, the words barely loud enough for anyone else to hear.

No one had expected this kind of just in case.

They scrambled through the brush together, branches whipping against their legs, thorns grabbing at their clothes. The woods blurred around them, sharp smells filling the air. Pine sap. Crushed leaves. Sweat and dirt and fear.

And then they saw her.

Jayda lay crumpled near the base of the trees, one arm twisted beneath her, one leg bent at an angle that made Mikki's stomach flip. Her braids were scattered across the ground like they had been dropped there. Her chest rose and fell in short, uneven bursts. Her eyes were open, blinking too fast, unfocused and glassy.

For a second, none of them moved.

Then Jayda sucked in a shaky breath and whispered, "It hurts."

The sound of her voice broke whatever spell had frozen them.

Zee dropped to her knees beside her, movements quick but careful. She did not touch Jayda right away. She had learned early that sometimes the most important thing was knowing when not to move something.

"I'm here," Zee said, her voice low and steady even as her hands hovered inches away. "Do not move. Okay? Do not move."

Mikki slid to the ground on Jayda's other side, her knees hitting dirt hard enough to sting. She pressed her hands flat against Jayda's shoulder, then froze, terrified she might make things worse.

"I am so sorry," she whispered, the words spilling out before she could stop them. "I checked it. I checked everything."

Toni stood a few steps back, her chest heaving as she tried to breathe through the panic clawing up her throat. Her eyes darted over Jayda's body, cataloging details she did not want to see. The scrape along Jayda's arm, red and gritty with dirt. The way her sneaker had come loose. The way the ground beneath her was pressed flat, like the earth itself had been punched.

"Toni," Zee said sharply. "Go get help. Now."

Toni did not move.

Her legs felt like they were made of sand. Heavy and useless.

"Toni," Zee said again, louder this time. "Run."

For a moment, Toni could not hear anything but the blood rushing in her ears. She wanted to stay. She wanted to kneel down and hold Jayda's hand and pretend this was something that could be fixed with tape and quiet words.

"Toni," Zee snapped, her voice cracking just once. "Run."

That did it.

Toni turned and ran.

Her sandals slapped against the dirt path as she tore through the woods, lungs burning, throat raw. Branches scraped her arms and legs, but she did not slow down. The only sound she could hear was her own breathing, loud and uneven, and the pounding of her heart.

This is real.

This is real.

This is real.

She burst out of the trees and onto the path that led toward the house, nearly tripping as the ground shifted from dirt to gravel. Her chest ached with every breath. Tears streamed down her face, blurring everything into streaks of light and shadow.

Behind her, the woods swallowed the sound of the broken zipline.

Ahead of her, the world was already changing.

Time did strange things after that.

It stretched and folded and twisted in on itself, moments dragging on forever while whole pieces of the afternoon disappeared completely. Mikki could not later remember how long she knelt there beside Jayda, hands shaking, trying to do something useful. She could not remember if she spoke out loud or if the words stayed trapped in her head.

Zee remembered everything.

She remembered the way Jayda's skin felt warm under her fingers when she finally dared to touch her wrist. She remembered counting her breaths, steady and quiet. In. Hold. Out. Hold. The way she'd practiced when her body needed reminding that it was safe.

Above them, the rope swayed, its frayed end twisting in the breeze like it was mocking them.

She hated that rope in that moment.

Hated the way it had betrayed them. Hated the way it had looked so strong just minutes before. Hated herself for trusting it.

"You are going to be okay," Zee said softly, though she did not know if it was true. "Help is coming."

Jayda tried to laugh and ended up coughing instead. Her face twisted, pain flashing sharp and bright across her features.

"Told you," she whispered. "Crash Queen."

Mikki squeezed her shoulder, careful not to press too hard. "Do not joke," she said, though her voice wobbled. "Please."

Jayda's eyes flicked toward her, trying to focus. "Hey," she said. "You good?"

The question hit Mikki like a slap.

"I am not the one on the ground," Mikki said. "Do not worry about me."

But Jayda kept looking at her, even through the pain. "You look like you are about to throw up."

Mikki huffed out a shaky breath that might have been a laugh if it did not sound so broken. "I might."

"Then sit down before you do."

Zee shot Mikki a look. "Listen to her."

Mikki obeyed, lowering herself fully onto the ground. Her legs felt weak, like they might give out at any second. She pressed her palms into the dirt, grounding herself in the smell and texture of the earth.

This was not how it was supposed to happen.

She had imagined so many versions of this moment. The cheer when Jayda landed. The laughter. The high fives. The way they would all crowd around, breathless and proud, already talking about the next run.

She had not imagined blood.

She had not imagined fear.

She had not imagined the awful, sinking certainty that this was her fault.

Sirens cut through the air in the distance.

The sound made Toni stumble to a stop on the porch as she shouted for Grandma Dot, words tumbling over each other, barely making sense. It made Mikki's heart lurch, relief and dread tangling together in her chest. It made Zee straighten her spine, bracing herself for what came next.

Help was coming.

That did not mean things would be okay.

Later, much later, people would ask questions.

They would want to know whose idea it was. They would ask who had been in charge. They would ask why four girls had been allowed to build something like that on their own.

Mikki would replay every step in her head, every measurement, every knot, every decision. Zee would lie awake at night, fingers twitching, tying invisible ropes in the dark. Toni would stop writing for a while, afraid that putting the story down on paper would make it too real. Jayda would carry the memory in her body, in the way she moved more carefully for a time, in the way she flinched when she heard ropes snap or wood crack.

But in this moment, none of that existed yet.
There was only the ground beneath them.
The broken rope above them.
And the truth settling quietly into all of their chests at once.
This was the moment everything tilted.
And nothing would move the same way again.

Chapter 1
One Week Ago

The yard looked the same as it always did.

The grass was cut unevenly, shorter near the porch where Grandma Dot liked it tidy and longer near the fence where nobody bothered. Mikki knew exactly why. Grandma Dot believed in clear edges. You could let things grow wild as long as you decided where they stopped.

The air hung heavy with late summer heat, the kind that made everything feel slower without actually stopping anything. Mikki liked that about summer afternoons. They gave you time to notice things before they demanded decisions. Somewhere down the block, a screen door slammed. A dog barked once and gave up. Cicadas buzzed from the trees, loud enough to press against the quiet without fully filling it.

Mikki noticed the yard the way she always did, in pieces.

The grass first. Where it thinned near the steps. Where it stayed thick and soft near the fence. Where the ground dipped just slightly, not enough to see unless you were looking for it. Grandma Dot said Mikki had "a mind that cataloged things." Mikki thought of it as responsibility that showed up early and never quite left.

She was staying at Grandma Dot's for the rest of the summer. That part had been decided quickly, with adult voices and careful phrasing that meant no one wanted to explain too much. Her mom's work schedule. Her dad's apartment not being ready yet. It was temporary. Everyone agreed on that word.

Mikki had learned that temporary still needed structure.

The porch belonged to her now in a way it hadn't before. She leaned against the rail without thinking, palm flat on the warm wood, fingers tracing the familiar groove where the paint always chipped. From here, she could see the whole yard without moving. That mattered.

The two trees stood across from each other like they always had.

Nothing special. Just trees.

One was thicker at the base, its trunk steady and wide. The other leaned slightly, branches reaching farther than they needed to, leaves catching the light at uneven angles. Mikki had noticed that lean weeks ago. She had thought about whether it had always been there or if she had only started paying attention once she knew she would be here longer.

She had not mentioned it.

The yard didn't ask her to.

For now, it was enough to know where everything was.

The girls were already there by the time Mikki pushed herself off the porch rail.

Not all at once. Not arriving together. Just present in the way people are when they've been drifting in and out of the same place long enough that no one remembers who came first. Grandma Dot's yard had always worked like that. It was open without being inviting. You didn't come because you were told to. You came because you knew you could stay.

Someone sat on the porch steps, shoes kicked off, toes brushing the warm wood. Someone leaned against the fence, one shoulder pressed into the chain links, bending them just enough to make a soft metallic sigh. Someone lay flat on the grass, arms folded behind her head, staring up at the sky like she was counting clouds or maybe not counting at all.

They talked about nothing that needed remembering.

A show one of them had half watched while scrolling on her phone. A teacher who talked too much and never noticed when people stopped listening. How summer still felt long even though school was coming, like time itself hadn't decided whether to speed up yet.

Mikki listened without joining in right away.

She stayed near the porch, one hand still grazing the rail, tracking the sound of their voices more than the words. She liked knowing where everyone was. Not because she didn't trust them, but because it made the space make sense. If she could picture where each person was standing or sitting, the yard stayed balanced.

She noticed how easily they fit into it.

Zee had claimed the fence like she always did, close to something solid. Toni hovered near the steps, notebook tucked under her arm even when she wasn't writing. Jayda had stretched out on the grass, body loose, limbs unguarded, like motion was something she could summon whenever she wanted and put away just as easily.

Mikki filed that away without comment.

The afternoon stretched. Heat pressed down without urgency. Cicadas buzzed from the trees, loud enough to fill the air but not loud enough to demand attention. Somewhere down the block, a screen door slammed. A dog barked once and gave up.

At some point, someone said, "You know what would be fun?"

The words weren't aimed at anyone in particular. They floated instead, light and casual, like they didn't need an answer to exist.

Nobody answered right away.

Someone laughed. Someone rolled onto her side, grass sticking to her elbow. Someone picked a blade of grass and snapped it between her fingers, the sound barely audible.

Mikki felt the sentence hover.

"I'm serious," the voice said again, not louder this time. Just steadier.

That was when the yard shifted.

Not physically. Nothing moved. But attention gathered, quiet and subtle, the way it does when several people start thinking in the same direction without agreeing to.

Mikki felt it before she saw it.

Her gaze lifted, following the invisible pull, and landed on the space between the trees.

The space between the trees wasn't far.

You could see it all at once without turning your head, which was part of what made it easy to miss. It didn't announce itself. It didn't look like anything waiting to happen. It was just there, open and ordinary, the kind of distance you crossed without thinking on your way to somewhere else.

Now, it held their attention.

Someone stood and paced it off, slow steps, heel to toe, counting under her breath or maybe not counting at all. Mikki counted anyway. She didn't mean to. The numbers lined themselves up without asking. Four steps. Five. The ground dipped slightly near the middle. She pictured it instantly, the way the space would feel under movement.

Someone else tipped her head back, squinting up through the leaves, tracking the branches the way you track clouds when you're deciding what they might turn into. Sunlight filtered through unevenly, catching on the leaves, breaking into patches that shifted as the breeze moved.

Someone reached out and touched the bark.

The sound was small. Skin against rough wood. Familiar. Anchoring.

Mikki watched how the branches responded to the wind. How they bent and then returned, never quite in the same position twice. She noticed the thickness of the trunks. The angle of the lean. The way the branches overlapped just enough to suggest connection without actually touching.

"It wouldn't even be that hard," someone said.

The sentence landed lightly, like a test.

Mikki felt her mouth open before she decided what she was going to say. Then she closed it again.

She hadn't finished thinking yet.

"Famous last words," someone else replied, but she was smiling, and the smile softened the warning into something that sounded like a joke.

They laughed.

The sound didn't travel far. It didn't echo or bounce or gather momentum. It settled quickly, thin and quick, like it was checking whether it belonged in the space before staying.

Mikki noticed that too.

No one said, *Let's do it.*

No one said, *That's a bad idea.*

The absence of decision sat with them, unchallenged.

They stayed where they were.

A breeze moved through the yard, lifting the leaves overhead just enough to send shadows sliding across the grass. The cicadas surged and then eased, their sound rising and falling without urgency. Somewhere nearby, a lawn mower coughed to life, stalled, then growled steadily again.

The world kept doing what it had been doing all along.

"Well," someone said after a while. "Not today."

"Yeah," someone else agreed. "Later."

Later felt close enough to touch.

Mikki leaned back against the porch rail again, grounding herself in the familiar line of it against her spine. She didn't argue. She didn't push. But she didn't let the moment disappear either.

She looked once more at the space between the trees.

The distance.

The angle.

What could fit there.

She didn't name it yet.

The yard held its shape. Nothing had changed. The space between the trees stayed exactly the same as it had been before anyone noticed it.

For now, that was enough.

They didn't mark the moment when the attention loosened.

It didn't snap or fade all at once. It simply thinned, the way heat does when a cloud drifts in front of the sun. Someone stopped pacing and dropped back down onto the grass. Someone else stepped away from the tree and brushed her hands on her shorts. The focus that had gathered between the trunks dissolved without anyone needing to name it.

Conversation slid sideways.

Someone brought up a movie trailer she'd seen that morning. Someone else complained about how summer homework shouldn't count if it was assigned during actual summer. Laughter came easier now, fuller, like it didn't have to test whether it belonged.

The yard returned to its familiar shape.

Mikki listened, half present, half somewhere else. She nodded at the right moments, laughed when the sound caught her off guard, but part of her stayed with the space they'd all just stopped looking at. She didn't turn back toward it again. She didn't need to. She could still see it.

Later always worked like that. It didn't demand attention. It waited.

She watched the way everyone settled back into themselves. Jayda rolled onto her stomach and propped her chin in her hands, legs swinging behind her without thought. Zee hooked her foot into the bottom of the fence, testing its give and then letting it be. Toni sat on the steps now, notebook still tucked away, listening more than she spoke.

Mikki noticed how easily the group slipped back into comfort.

That, too, felt important.

"Well," someone said eventually, stretching the word out like it didn't have a clear destination. "I'm starving."

"That's not a plan," someone else replied. "That's a complaint."

"It can be both," Jayda said, grinning.

They laughed again, louder this time. The sound carried farther, spilling past the yard, unbothered by whether it belonged.

Mikki pushed herself off the porch rail and joined them on the steps, sitting close enough that their shoulders nearly touched. She liked being able to feel the warmth of other people without having to say anything about it. The closeness made the space feel contained again, like the yard knew where it ended.

She thought about Grandma Dot inside the house, moving through the kitchen with steady purpose, trusting them to occupy the space without supervision. That trust felt heavier than rules would have.

Temporary, Mikki reminded herself.

But temporary still needed care.

Someone stood. Someone else followed. The group drifted, easy and unstructured, toward snacks and shade and whatever came next. The idea that had hovered between the trees didn't follow them inside.

It stayed behind.

The yard held it without changing shape.

Mikki glanced back once, just before stepping through the door.

Not because she was worried.

Because she wanted to remember exactly how it looked before anything happened.

The space between the trees stayed open. Ordinary. Unclaimed.

For now, that was enough.

The house swallowed the sound when they went inside.

The screen door slapped shut behind them, cutting off the cicadas mid-pulse. Cool air settled over Mikki's skin, lifting the heaviness of the afternoon without erasing it completely. The kitchen smelled like whatever Grandma Dot had been making earlier, something warm and familiar that didn't need identifying.

They spread out the way they always did. Someone leaned against the counter. Someone opened the fridge and stared into it like answers might appear if she waited long enough. Someone else perched on a stool, swinging her legs and talking all at once.

Mikki moved more slowly.

She poured herself a glass of water and stood near the sink, watching the way the surface rippled as she set it down. She drank half, then the rest, letting the coolness ground her. Inside, the house felt smaller than the yard, contained in a way that made it easier to hold things steady.

Conversation overlapped. Snacks were claimed and argued over. Someone complained about having to leave soon. Someone else said they could stay a little longer.

Mikki listened, nodded, responded when she needed to.

But part of her stayed outside.

Not with the trees exactly. With the idea of them. With the distance she had already measured without trying. With the way the branches had bent and returned, the way the space between them had felt balanced, almost intentional.

She didn't think *zipline*.

She thought *if*.

If something were stretched between them.

If weight moved through that space.

If speed met structure.

She didn't go any further than that.

Mikki had learned, long before this summer, that ideas could be just as dangerous as actions if you let them run too far ahead.

She liked to keep hers close, contained, examined from different angles before she trusted them.

Grandma Dot passed through the kitchen then, setting a bowl on the table without asking who wanted it. She gave Mikki a look as she went by, brief and knowing, the kind that said *I see you* without making a big deal of it.

Mikki held that look longer than she held the glass.

The afternoon wore on. The heat outside softened. Shadows shifted across the floor. Eventually, shoes were pulled back on and plans were made to meet up again tomorrow, or maybe the next day, or sometime soon.

Later, always later.

They left in pairs and singles, voices trailing down the sidewalk until the house settled into its quieter shape again. Mikki watched from the doorway until the last of them disappeared, then closed the door gently behind her.

The silence that followed wasn't empty.

She walked back toward the window that faced the yard and looked out once more. The trees stood exactly where they had before. The space between them waited without asking for anything.

Mikki rested her hand against the glass.

Not to claim it.

Just to remember it.

She turned away without opening the door.

The idea stayed with her, folded neatly, not acted on, not dismissed.

Some things didn't need to be built right away to matter.

She would learn later how true that was.

Later that night, the yard looked different.

Not changed. Just quieter.

Mikki stood at the back window with the lights off behind her, watching the darkness settle into the shapes she already knew. The grass disappeared first, edges softening until it blended into shadow. The fence held longer, its line still visible if you knew where to look. The trees remained last, their outlines steady against the dim sky, branches layered like they always were.

The space between them was harder to see now.

That made Mikki notice it more.

Inside, the house had settled into its evening sounds. Grandma Dot's television murmured low in the other room. Pipes clicked once and then went still. Somewhere down the block, a car passed, tires humming briefly before fading.

Mikki stayed where she was.

She thought again about the way the afternoon had unfolded. How the idea had arrived without announcement. How no one had pushed it forward. How easily it might have slipped away if she let it.

She didn't feel urgency.

That surprised her.

Usually, once something took shape in her head, it pressed for completion. It demanded planning, measuring, checking. Tonight, it sat quietly, waiting to be understood before it asked to be acted on.

She let it.

Tomorrow, the yard would look the same. The grass would still be uneven. The porch rail would still carry the warmth of the day. The trees would stand where they always had.

Nothing would be different yet.

That felt important.

Mikki stepped back from the window and turned off the kitchen light, moving through the house without rushing. She paused once at the hallway, listening, then continued toward her room.

The idea stayed with her.

Not loud.

Not insistent.

Just present.

Before she closed her door, Mikki glanced back one last time, not at the yard itself but at the reflection of the window in the dark glass. She saw her own outline there, steady and unmoving.

She didn't know yet what would come of the space between the trees.

She only knew she would not forget it.

And that, for now, was enough.

Chapter 2
Zee's Jar of String

Zahara Johnson had always been a quiet girl in a world that did not know how to be still.

Even now, the sound of summer pressed in from every direction, a constant, overlapping hum that never fully faded. The cicadas still screeched from the trees, loud and mechanical, as if tiny engines were hidden beneath the bark, but beneath them the crickets had begun to edge in, their uneven chorus rising and falling like breath. Wind chimes clinked from porches up and down the street, thin notes tangling together in the heat. Somewhere nearby, a lawn mower growled and stalled and growled again. Birds shouted from the branches like they were arguing over something important, and farther off, a radio played music with bass so deep it rumbled in your chest.

Zee had learned that even silence had a sound if you listened closely enough.

She did not mind the noise of nature. That kind of loud made room for you. It did not demand answers or explanations. It did not ask you to be anything other than present. The other kind of noise, though, the voices and questions and expectations that came from people, that was harder. Those sounds crowded in on her thoughts, pressed against her ribs, made her want to disappear into the edges of things.

Sometimes she just wanted a place where she did not have to explain why she liked bugs more than Barbies. Why she would rather fix something broken than talk about how she felt. Why quiet felt safer than being seen.

When her family moved in next door to Grandma Dot's house, it was mid-July, and the air felt like thick soup. The sun bounced off the driveway so brightly it burned her eyes even through the car window. Zee sat in the backseat of the minivan, hugging her backpack to her chest like it might float away if she let go. Her little brother snored beside her, mouth open, completely unbothered by the chaos of moving. In the front seat, her parents argued gently about whether the moving truck would beat them there.

Zee barely heard them.

All she could think was, I don't want to start over again.

She had moved three times in the last four years. Every move came with new hallways to memorize, new rules to follow, new faces that asked the same questions in slightly different ways.

Why are you so quiet.

Why don't you smile more.

What's in that jar.

She never knew how to answer in a way that made sense to anyone else.

The jar was not just string and wire.

It was the story of the day her neighbor's cat got stuck in a garden trellis and no one could figure out how to get it free. Zee had stood back and watched, watched the adults panic and pull and shout over each other. Someone tried forcing the metal apart. Someone else yelled about calling animal control. The cat hissed and clawed, eyes wide with fear, its back leg twisted at an angle that made Zee's stomach hurt just looking at it.

She had seen the problem almost immediately.

The trellis was held together with screws, old and rusted but still intact. Pulling harder would only make things worse. Everyone was focused on force. They were missing the fix.

Zee had walked back into her house and grabbed her lunchbox from the counter. Inside was a plastic spoon she had sharpened against the sidewalk the day before, just to see if she could. She knelt beside the trellis, hands shaking as she slid the spoon under one of the screws and twisted slowly.

It took longer than she expected. Her wrist hurt. Her palms burned.

But eventually, the screw loosened enough for the metal to bend.

The cat slipped free and bolted without a backward glance.

The adults stared at her like she had performed a magic trick.

After that, she started keeping things.

Not because she liked clutter.

Because sometimes things broke. And sometimes, she could fix them. She just needed the right pieces.

That was how the jar was born.

A few days later, Zee found herself sitting cross legged in the shade of Grandma Dot's backyard, the jar balanced carefully between her knees, it felt like an extension of her. Sunlight filtered through the leaves overhead, catching on the glass and turning it into something almost magical. Inside, the contents shifted gently when she moved, bits of metal and string knocking together softly, a quiet language only she understood.

To anyone else, it probably looked like junk.

To Zee, it was a safety net.

She unscrewed the lid slowly and reached inside, fingers brushing familiar shapes. A twist-tie from a bread bag. A bent paper clip she had straightened and bent again more times than she could count. Two rubber bands, one thick and stubborn, the other thin and fragile. A strip of Velcro folded neatly in half. A safety pin. A small coil of twine. The kitten Band-Aid, still unused, tucked against the glass like a promise.

She did not take anything out yet.

She just needed to know it was all still there.

If it's there, I'm okay, she told herself.

That was when she heard footsteps near the woods.

Zee looked up just as another girl crouched nearby, eyes locked on something in the grass.

"Don't touch him," the girl shouted suddenly, urgency sharp in her voice. "You could hurt him worse."

Zee froze, then softened her hands.

"I know," she said quietly.

The girl blinked. "Wait. What is that."

Zee did not answer. She was already opening the jar.

Zee did not look up right away.

She knelt in the grass, the jar open beside her knee, her focus narrowed to the small, frantic body trapped in front of her. The frog's skin was slick and green, its sides fluttering too fast as it struggled against the jagged aluminum edge of the crushed soda can. Every kick scraped metal against skin, a sharp sound that made Zee's chest tighten.

She reached into the jar and pulled out a thin piece of wire, bending it gently between her fingers. Her movements were careful, deliberate. She did not rush. Rushing was how things broke.

Behind her, the other girl hovered, hands clenched into fists at her sides.

"I didn't mean you," the girl said quickly. "I just didn't want him hurt."

Zee nodded once. "I know."

She slid the wire under the torn lip of the can and began to pry it back, inch by inch. The metal resisted at first, then slowly gave way with a soft groan. Zee paused when the frog kicked again, waiting until it stilled before continuing.

The girl let out a breath she had clearly been holding.

"You're really good at that," she said.

Zee shrugged, though her cheeks warmed. "He just needs space."

The wire bent a little more. The opening widened. The frog wriggled free suddenly, launching itself from Zee's hands and disappearing into the brush with a splash of leaves and dirt.

For a moment, everything went quiet.

Then the girl exploded.

"Oh my gosh," she shouted, throwing both arms in the air. "Did you see that. You literally just saved his whole life. That was amazing. Like better than the Super Bowl amazing."

Zee stared at her, unsure what to do with that much enthusiasm aimed directly at her.

"I mean it," the girl went on, pacing in a tight circle. "That was surgical. You didn't even hesitate. What's your name."

"Zahara," Zee said softly. "But people call me Zee."

"Well, Zee," the girl said, grinning wide. "You just earned yourself a lifetime membership to my team."

Zee blinked. "Your team."

"Yeah," the girl said. "I'm Mikki."

She stuck out her hand like they were sealing a deal.

Zee hesitated for half a second, then shook it.

The feeling that settled in her chest surprised her. It was not loud or overwhelming. It was small and steady, like something clicking into place.

Maybe she did not have to walk the edges here.

That feeling followed her now, days later, as she moved through Grandma Dot's backyard with the others. The frog incident had turned into introductions, which had turned into conversations, which had turned into this. Rope and ladders and notebooks and laughter that felt easy instead of forced.

Zee set the jar down near the base of the oak and stood, brushing dirt from her knees.

"Anchor Zee," Toni repeated, testing the words like she was already shaping them into sentences.

Zee pretended to inspect the rope again, but the name echoed anyway.

Anchor meant steady. It meant holding things in place. It meant being trusted with weight.

She liked that.

They worked through the afternoon, the sun shifting slowly overhead. Mikki talked constantly, explaining her ideas out loud as if saying them made them more real. She measured distances with long strides, adjusted angles, erased and rewrote numbers in her notebook.

"If the drop is gradual enough," Mikki said, pacing beneath the rope, "the speed stays controlled. It's just physics."

Jayda snorted from the grass. "That's what everyone says right before something goes wrong."

Mikki rolled her eyes. "You're not even up there yet."

"Yet," Jayda echoed, grinning.

Zee climbed the ladder again, careful with each rung. The wood creaked under her weight, a sound she noted and filed away. At the branch, she tested the knot again, fingers tracing the loops, checking for slippage.

It held.

Still, she retied it.

"You already checked that," Jayda called up.

"I know," Zee said. "I'm checking it again."

Mikki nodded approvingly. "Redundancy is smart."

That word settled next to anchor in Zee's mind.

Smart. Useful. Needed.

She descended the ladder and reached for the jar again, adjusting the position of the rope where it rubbed against the bark. She slid a strip of fabric beneath it, cushioning the contact point.

"What's that for," Toni asked.

"Friction," Zee said. "It can wear things down faster than you think."

Toni's eyes lit up. "I'm writing that."

"Write the part where nothing breaks," Jayda said. "That's the important part."

Zee smiled faintly.

As the afternoon stretched on, the jar became a constant companion. Zee reached for it without thinking, pulling out small solutions to problems no one else noticed. A twist tie to secure a loose end. Velcro to keep a strap from sliding. Twine to reinforce a temporary hold.

Each fix was small.

Together, they mattered.

By late afternoon, after hours of work shadows stretched long across the yard. The rope sagged slightly under its own weight, but held firm when Zee pulled with both hands.

Mikki clapped once. "Okay. I think we're getting somewhere."

Jayda sat up, brushing grass from her arms. "Does this mean I get to jump yet."

"Not today," Mikki said. "We're still testing."

Jayda groaned dramatically and flopped back down. "You engineers are cruel."

Zee packed the jar back into her backpack carefully, tucking it in like something breakable. As she zipped it closed, her fingers brushed the kitten bandaid again.

She paused.

She did not know why that small square of fabric kept catching her attention. It had always been there. It had never mattered before.

She pushed the thought aside.

As they cleaned up, Zee glanced once more at the space beneath the rope. The ground looked ordinary. Soft dirt. Scattered leaves. Nothing threatening.

Still, something twisted low in her stomach.

She shook her head.

You checked everything, she told herself. You always do.

That night, lying in bed in her new room, Zee stared up at the ceiling long after the house went quiet. Boxes still lined one wall, half unpacked, but the jar sat on the nightstand within reach.

She replayed the day in her mind.

The frog.

Mikki's grin.

Toni's careful watching.

Jayda's fearless jokes.

The rope holding steady under her hands.

Zee turned onto her side and reached out, fingers brushing the cool glass.

Just in case, she thought.

She did not know yet how much that phrase would matter.

Not yet.

Chapter 3
Jayda the Crash Queen

Jayda Marie Ellis had learned how to take up space before anyone ever told her she was taking up too much of it.

She did it with sound first. With laughter that rang out sharp and sudden, the kind that turned heads whether people wanted it to or not. With sneakers that lit up when she walked, flashing bright colors against sidewalks and grass and concrete, announcing her presence before her voice ever had to. With beads at the ends of her braids that clicked together every time she moved, a steady reminder that she was there, that she could not be ignored.

Being loud meant being seen. Being seen meant being safe.

Jayda had decided that a long time ago, back when teachers sighed before they even finished calling her name, back when adults told her to calm down without ever asking why she was wound so tight to begin with. Loud was armor. Loud was control. Loud meant nobody got to decide who she was for her.

That afternoon, she burst through the side gate of Grandma Dot's yard like she owned it, one hand shoving the metal open with a loud rattle. Her shirt was bright white, the words I BREAK RULES, NOT BONES stretched across her chest. Her hands went straight to her hips as she scanned the scene in front of her.

"What is all this?" she demanded.

Mikki barely looked up from her notebook, pencil moving fast. Zee was crouched near the oak tree, fingers tight around a rope, eyes focused like the world might fall apart if she blinked at the wrong moment. Toni sat on the porch steps with her notebook balanced on her knees, already watching Jayda like she was something worth writing down.

Jayda took it all in. The ladder leaning against the tree. The rope stretched between branches. The way nobody was joking around.

"Nerd stuff," she said automatically.

Mikki stood and brushed her hands on her shorts. "We're building something."

Jayda snorted. "Looks like y'all about to hurt yourselves."

"Probably," Mikki said, calm as ever. "You want to help?"

That made Jayda pause.

She had expected a clapback. A joke. Someone telling her to keep it moving. Instead, Mikki looked at her like she already belonged there, like her being in the yard was normal.

"You didn't even ask," Jayda said.

"I just did."

Jayda laughed, loud and sharp, but something inside her shifted. She crossed her arms, weight settling into one hip. "I don't do rope stuff."

Zee spoke without looking up. "You don't have to."

Jayda turned toward her. "Then what do I do?"

"You jump," Mikki said.

Jayda followed Mikki's finger up the oak tree, eyes tracing the rope stretched across the yard. She pictured herself there for half a second. The height. The air. The rush. Her stomach flipped before she could stop it.

She covered it fast. "I'm not trying to break my neck."

"We have plans," Mikki said. "And Zee."

Zee finally looked up, her gaze steady. "I tie good knots."

Jayda studied her for a beat, then smiled. "I like her."

Toni cleared her throat. "And I document things."

Jayda laughed again. "Of course you do."

She took a few steps closer, circling the rope like she was sizing it up. She tugged on it lightly. It barely moved.

"Okay," she said slowly. "Say I help. What does that make me?"

"Our tester," Mikki said without hesitation.

Jayda grinned. "Say less."

She showed up the next day like she had always been part of the plan. Hair pulled into two puffballs, beads clicking with every step. Backpack thudding onto the porch steps, snacks rattling inside.

"So," she announced, stretching her arms overhead. "What are we building today, builders?"

Mikki tossed her a measuring tape. Jayda caught it easily, spinning it once around her finger.

"Bet."

Jayda surprised herself with how much she liked it. Carrying boards. Holding the ladder steady while Zee climbed. Listening to Mikki explain angles and tension like it actually mattered.

"How much weight can it hold?" she asked at one point, eyeing the rope.

Mikki flipped through her notes. "More than you."

Jayda gasped. "Rude."

"It's math."

Jayda shrugged. "Math hates me too."

They laughed, but Jayda kept watching. She noticed how Zee tested every knot twice. How Mikki stopped and remeasured instead of rushing. How Toni wrote everything down like she was afraid the moment might disappear if she didn't catch it.

It made Jayda feel something she wasn't used to feeling.

Trusted.

Nobody expected her to mess this up. Nobody hovered, waiting for her to fail. That was new.

The first time they suggested she try the setup, Jayda didn't say yes right away. The harness was padded carefully. Hay bales were stacked beneath the line.

"You sure?" she asked, tightening the strap.

Zee nodded. "I checked it."

Mikki added, "And I checked her check."

Jayda laughed. "That sounds official."

Toni lifted her phone. "Crash Queen, you ready?"

Crash Queen.

The name settled somewhere deep in Jayda's chest. A joke, sure. But also something else. Something that belonged to her.

She climbed onto the stump. It wasn't high. Just enough to matter. The yard felt quieter all of a sudden. Leaves rustled overhead. The air smelled like sun and dirt and wood.

Jayda took a breath.

Then she jumped.

The rope held.

She flew.

For a few wild seconds, the world dropped away. The ground blurred beneath her. Wind pushed against her face, lifting her braids behind her. She screamed, not from fear, but from joy, from movement, from the feeling of being uncontained.

She landed hard but safe, hay exploding around her as she rolled and laughed until her sides hurt.

"That," she gasped, pushing herself up, "was incredible."

Mikki shook her head. "You are out of your mind."

"You're welcome," Jayda said. "Now you know it works."

Later, when the sun dipped low and the yard emptied out, Jayda lingered a little longer than she meant to. She sat on the porch steps, kicking her heels against the wood, watching Zee carefully coil rope back into neat loops.

"You always this serious?" Jayda asked.

Zee shrugged. "Someone has to be."

Jayda nodded, understanding more than she expected to. Loud and careful. Fearless and steady. Maybe they balanced each other.

That night, Jayda lay on her bed with the window open, crickets singing into the dark. The streetlight outside molded soft shapes across her ceiling.

She thought about the jump. About the way the girls had looked at her afterward. Not like she was trouble. Not like she was too much.

Like she mattered.

Crash Queen, she thought.

Maybe crashing didn't mean failing.

Maybe it just meant you were brave enough to leap first.

Jayda did not tell anyone how long she sat there that night, staring at the ceiling while the fan rattled above her head. She did not tell them how her legs still buzzed faintly, like the jump had left something electric behind. She definitely did not tell them how quiet her room felt once the noise of the day faded away.

Jayda was not used to quiet.

Her house was usually loud, even when nobody was talking. The television hummed from the living room. Someone's phone buzzed with notifications that never seemed to stop. The neighbor's dog barked at nothing like it was its job. Quiet only showed up late, when everyone else had gone to sleep and there was nothing left to distract her.

That was when thoughts got bold.

She rolled onto her side and stared at the wall, the glow from the streetlight sneaking through the blinds in thin stripes. Her braids were piled up on her pillow, beads cold against her neck. She reached up and tugged one loose, rolling it between her fingers.

Crash Queen.

She smiled at the name, but the smile didn't last. The truth was, she had been called worse things before. Loud. Extra. Too much. Teachers liked to say her name with a sigh, like it came with instructions she never quite followed. Adults liked to say she had potential, which always sounded like code for *someday you'll calm down.*

Jayda hated that word. *Potential.*

It felt like waiting. Like holding your breath for a version of yourself that might never show up.

What she liked about Grandma Dot's backyard was that nobody asked her to be quieter. Nobody told her to slow down or lower her voice. They let her laugh. Let her move. Let her jump without flinching first.

That mattered more than she wanted to admit.

The next afternoon, she showed up early on purpose.

She hopped the side gate instead of opening it, landing lightly on the grass like she'd done it a hundred times before. Mikki was already there, sitting cross legged with her notebook open, pencil tucked behind her ear. Zee was kneeling near the base of the oak tree, fingers busy with rope. Toni sat nearby, scribbling fast, pausing every so often to look up and watch.

Jayda stopped just inside the yard and took it all in.

Nobody jumped at the sound of her landing. Nobody looked annoyed. Mikki just glanced up and grinned.

"You're early," Mikki said.

Jayda shrugged. "Didn't have nothing else to do."

That was not entirely true. She could have stayed home. Could have slept in. Could have scrolled on her phone until her thumb cramped. But something about this place pulled at her. Something about the way they were building something together made the rest of the day feel less important.

She dropped her backpack near the porch and wandered over to Zee, watching her work.

"You ever mess up a knot?" Jayda asked.

Zee did not look up. "Sometimes."

Jayda raised an eyebrow. "That's not comforting."

Zee finally glanced at her. "I mess up less when I take my time."

Jayda nodded slowly. That made sense.

She watched Zee's hands move, steady and deliberate. No rush. No panic. Just focus. Jayda realized then that she had never really learned how to slow down like that. Everything she did was fast or loud or both. Slowing down felt like giving doubt a chance to catch her.

Still, she stayed.

Mikki called her over a little while later to help measure distance between the trees. Jayda held the end of the tape while Mikki paced it out, counting softly under her breath.

"Hold it tight," Mikki said.

"I am," Jayda replied, pulling it taut.

Mikki smiled. "You always this serious?"

Jayda snorted. "Only when it matters."

Mikki looked at her for a second longer than necessary, like she was filing that away for later.

They worked like that for hours. Measuring. Adjusting. Testing. Laughing when something slipped or a number got crossed out. Toni asked questions sometimes, not about the build but about them.

"Why that tree?"
"Why that angle?"
"Why here?"

Jayda liked that Toni listened when they answered. She liked that Toni wrote it all down, even the jokes, like none of it was wasted.

At one point, Mikki stepped back and wiped her forehead. "Okay," she said. "I think we're good for today."

Jayda felt a strange flicker of disappointment. She hid it by stretching her arms over her head.

"So what now?" she asked.

"Now we stop before we rush," Zee said.

Jayda tilted her head. "You really don't like rushing."

Zee shook her head. "Rushing breaks things."

Jayda laughed. "Story of my life."

Zee looked at her then, really looked at her, like she was trying to understand something beneath the joke. Jayda held her gaze, surprised when she didn't feel the urge to look away first.

That night, Jayda dreamed she was running.

Not away from anything. Not toward anything either. Just running, fast and free, the ground solid beneath her feet. When she woke up, her heart was steady, not racing like it usually did after dreams.

The next few days settled into a rhythm. Show up. Build a little more. Talk a little longer. Laugh louder. Jayda found herself waiting for afternoons instead of counting them down.

She started bringing extra snacks. Started staying later. Started noticing small things, like how Mikki always double checked numbers even when she was sure, or how Toni chewed the end of her pencil when she was thinking, or how Zee touched the rope almost absentmindedly, like it was something alive.

One afternoon, while Mikki and Toni were arguing quietly about whether documentation counted as proof, Jayda sat beside Zee in the shade.

"You move a lot," Jayda said suddenly.

Zee glanced at her. "What."

"Like houses. Neighborhoods. Stuff like that."

Zee hesitated, then nodded. "Yeah."

Jayda kicked at the dirt with her sneaker. "That sucks."

Zee shrugged. "You get used to it."

Jayda frowned. "I don't want to get used to leaving places."

Zee said nothing, but the silence between them felt heavier than before.

Jayda filled it the only way she knew how. "Well," she said, forcing a grin, "you stuck with us for now. So deal with it."

Zee smiled, small but real.

That night, Jayda lay awake again, but this time she wasn't staring at the ceiling. She was smiling into the dark.

She thought about how it felt to be part of something that wasn't just loud or flashy. Something that needed her, not because she was fearless, but because she showed up.

Crash Queen, she thought again.

Maybe the name didn't mean what she used to think it did.

Maybe crashing wasn't about breaking things.

Maybe it was about landing and getting back up.

Jayda did not tell anyone about the way her chest felt lighter after a few days of showing up. She did not have the language for it anyway. It was not happiness exactly. It was not excitement either. It was more like relief, the kind you feel when you realize you have been holding something heavy for a long time without noticing.

She noticed it in small ways first.

She stopped checking her phone every few minutes while she was in the yard. She stopped scanning the street for people she knew, or people she thought might judge her for being there. She even stopped cracking jokes just to fill the space when things went quiet. The quiet did not feel dangerous here. It felt earned.

One afternoon, while they took a break in the shade, Mikki leaned back on her elbows and stared up at the sky. "You ever think about what you'd do if school wasn't a thing," she asked, like it had just occurred to her.

Jayda snorted. "Sleep. All day."

Toni smiled but kept writing. "That's not an answer."

"It is if you tired," Jayda said.

Zee shrugged. "I'd fix stuff."

Jayda looked at her. "Like what."

"Anything that's broken," Zee said. "Stuff people give up on."

Jayda felt something twist in her chest at that. She did not say anything, but she understood it. Being given up on felt familiar.

Mikki turned her head toward Jayda. "What about you."

Jayda opened her mouth automatically, ready with something loud and careless. Something easy. But the words did not come right away.

"I don't know," she said finally.

That surprised all of them, including her.

She kicked at the dirt, watching dust puff up around her sneaker. "I guess... I like moving. I like feeling like I'm not stuck."

Mikki nodded slowly, like that made sense. "You don't seem stuck."

Jayda laughed, sharp and quick. "That's because I don't let people see when I am."

Nobody teased her for that. Nobody tried to soften it or turn it into a joke. Toni's pencil paused, just for a second, before she kept writing.

That night, Jayda went home and stared at herself in the mirror longer than usual. She tilted her head, studying her own face. The confidence. The bravado. The girl everyone thought they knew.

"Crash Queen," she said out loud.

The name still fit. But it felt different now. Less like a warning. More like a badge.

The next day, she caught herself arriving early again. She leaned against the fence and watched Mikki and Zee work together, the quiet efficiency between them. She realized something then that made her stomach flutter in a way that had nothing to do with jumping or moving fast.

They trusted her.

Not because she was fearless. Not because she was loud. But because she showed up. Because she listened when it mattered. Because she did the work.

That was new.

Jayda had always been chosen last for serious things. First for blame. First for jokes. First for being told to calm down. Here, she was chosen on purpose.

When Toni asked if she could write her nickname in the notebook, Jayda hesitated for half a second.

"Spell it right," she said.

Toni smiled. "I always do."

As the sun dipped lower and shadows stretched across the yard, Jayda helped coil rope and stack tools. She worked slower than usual, deliberate, careful not to rush. When she finished, she sat on the porch steps and let her legs dangle, listening to the sounds of the neighborhood settle into evening.

For once, she did not feel like running anywhere else.

She felt rooted.

Later, lying in bed, Jayda thought about how strange it was that something so simple could change the way a day felt. Showing up. Being needed. Being trusted without having to perform first.

She rolled onto her side, staring at the wall, a small smile pulling at her mouth.

Crash Queen, she thought again.

Maybe crashing was not about falling apart.

Maybe it was about hitting the ground and realizing you were still standing.

And for the first time, that idea did not scare her at all.

Chapter 4
Toni's Notebook

Toni Belle Greene had learned how to disappear without actually going anywhere.

She could sit in a room full of people and feel like she was standing just outside of it, watching through a window no one else could see. Teachers passed over her raised hand without noticing it was there. Classmates borrowed pencils from her desk and returned them without ever making eye contact. Even adults sometimes talked around her instead of to her, their voices flowing above her head like she was part of the furniture.

It was not that Toni had nothing to say.

It was the opposite.

Her thoughts were constant, layered, crowded. They filled her head from the moment she woke up until long after the house went quiet at night. Ideas bloomed without warning. Stories formed while she brushed her teeth, while she counted steps on the stairs, while she stared at the back of someone else's shirt in line at the store. Characters argued with each other in her mind. Scenes unfolded fully formed, like movies she could pause and rewind at will.

Speaking felt risky.

Once words left her mouth, they were no longer hers. They could be interrupted, misunderstood, laughed at, or ignored. Choosing which thought to say out loud felt impossible, like trying to pick a single shell from an entire beach and hoping it explained the ocean.

So Toni learned another way.

She learned how to be quiet without being empty. How to listen instead of jump in. How to nod at the right moments so people assumed she agreed. How to make herself smaller when rooms felt too loud or expectations pressed too close. Disappearing became a skill. A kind of safety.

At school, it meant sitting near the back of the classroom where she could see everyone without being seen herself. It meant finishing group projects quietly and letting louder voices take credit because correcting them felt like too much effort. It meant teachers writing comments like "thoughtful" and "sweet" on her report cards without ever asking what she thought about anything that mattered.

At home, it meant hovering near the edges of conversations, absorbing stories instead of sharing her own. Her parents loved her, she knew that, but love did not always translate into attention. They asked about grades and chores and whether she had eaten dinner. They did not ask about the worlds she carried around inside her.

Toni did not blame them.

Invisible people learned early that attention was something you earned by being loud or impressive or demanding. Toni was none of those things. She was observant. She noticed the way people's voices changed when they were tired. She noticed when laughter sounded forced. She noticed when someone wanted to be asked a question but did not know how to ask for it.

She noticed everything.

That noticing became its own kind of weight.

By the time she found Grandma Dot's backyard and the three girls who filled it with plans and noise and motion, Toni was already used to standing slightly apart, watching instead of joining. Even when she sat with them, knees pulled close, notebook resting on her lap, she felt like the quiet space between notes in a song. Necessary, maybe, but rarely acknowledged.

And yet, something about this place made disappearing harder.

Maybe it was the way Mikki talked through her ideas out loud, messy and confident, like thinking was something you were supposed to share. Maybe it was the way Zee worked in careful silence without apologizing for it. Maybe it was Jayda's laughter, sharp and fearless, daring the world to deal with her exactly as she was.

Toni did not know yet where she fit among them.

All she knew was that for the first time in a long while, being invisible felt less like protection and more like a choice she might not want to keep making forever.

She tightened her grip on the notebook in her lap and kept watching, words stacking quietly inside her, waiting.

The notebook was the place Toni put everything she could not say out loud.

It was thick and spiral bound, heavy enough that it felt reassuring in her hands. The cover was a shimmery pink that caught the light just enough to feel special without being flashy. Puffy glitter stickers dotted the front, some peeling at the edges from being pressed down and lifted up too many times. Across the center, the word IMAGINE was hot glued in crooked silver letters, one rhinestone missing from the I.

Toni liked that missing stone.

It reminded her that nothing she loved was supposed to be perfect. Just honest.

She had gotten the notebook years ago, a back to school purchase that had been meant for math notes or vocabulary lists. Instead, it became something else almost immediately. The first page held a story she never finished, about a girl who could turn invisible whenever she wanted but slowly forgot how to turn back. The next pages filled quickly after that, stories spilling over margins, arrows pointing to rewrites, whole paragraphs scratched out and rewritten sideways along the edge.

Inside, the pages were full.

Not neat. Not organized. Just full.

Princesses who built robots instead of waiting to be rescued. Talking animals who solved mysteries when adults missed the obvious clues. A lonely girl who lived on the moon and planted stars in the ground like seeds, hoping one day they would grow bright enough to light her way home.

Some days, Toni wrote scenes like they were movies, all dialogue and movement and noise. Other days, she wrote quiet things. Single lines. Questions she did not know how to ask anyone else. Lists of words that felt important even if she could not explain why.

Her handwriting changed with her mood. When she was calm, the letters were round and careful, evenly spaced. When she was excited, the words leaned forward, racing each other across the page. When she was scared or unsure, the lines tightened near the bottom, letters shrinking as if they were trying to hide.

The notebook noticed everything, even when no one else did.

No one had ever really read it.

Teachers praised her essays but never asked about the stories. They circled grammar mistakes and wrote comments like "strong imagery" without asking where the images came from. Her mom flipped through a few pages once, smiled, and said writing was a nice hobby, the same way she talked about coloring or puzzles, something pleasant but temporary.

Kids at school sometimes peeked over her shoulder and asked if she was writing about them, their tone half teasing, half suspicious. Toni always closed the notebook then, snapping it shut before anyone could get close enough to misunderstand.

Some things were hers.

The notebook was proof that her thoughts existed, even if she did not say them. Proof that she was more than quiet. Proof that the worlds inside her were real, even if they only lived on paper.

That afternoon in Grandma Dot's backyard, with the hum of summer all around them, Toni rested the notebook on her lap and traced the edge of the cover with her thumb. The girls talked and moved and planned, their voices overlapping in a way that usually made her shrink back.

Instead, she opened to a blank page.

The pencil hovered for a moment, then touched down.

She began to write, letting the words go where they wanted, trusting that the notebook would hold them the way it always had.

The first time Mikki asked to see Toni's notebook, Toni thought she had misheard her.

They had been sitting outside Toni's apartment building on the curb, the concrete still warm from the sun. The air felt heavy and restless, the kind of afternoon where thunder lingered somewhere far away but never quite arrived. Toni had her notebook balanced on her knees, pencil moving without much thought as she sketched the outline of a castle made of glass and vines. Every window glowed softly, even though the sun was still out. She liked drawing things that looked fragile but held themselves together anyway.

Mikki's bike squeaked as she skidded to a stop nearby.

Toni did not look up right away. She recognized the sound. Mikki's bike always announced her before she did, like it could not wait its turn.

"Whatcha doing?" Mikki asked, already hopping off before the bike fully stopped.

"Nothing," Toni said automatically, angling the notebook away with her elbow.

Mikki flopped down beside her, heat radiating off her like she had been riding fast. A braid poked out from the back of her helmet, fraying at the edges, like it had barely survived the trip.

"You always say that," Mikki said. "But you always look like you're solving something."

Toni shrugged, eyes fixed on the page. "It's just dumb stuff."

Mikki leaned closer, peering at the corner of the notebook she could still see. "Can I look?"

The question landed heavier than Toni expected.

She finally looked up. "You want to?"

Mikki blinked, confused. "Yeah. Why not?"

No one had ever said it like that before. Casual. Certain. Like it was the most natural thing in the world to want to see what Toni was working on. Not a favor. Not a joke. Not a test.

Just interest.

Toni's fingers tightened around the notebook. Her heart thudded hard enough that she was sure Mikki could hear it.

If she laughs, Toni thought, I'll never show anyone again.

She stared down at the page. At the careful lines. At the parts of herself she usually kept hidden. Slowly, like she was handing over something fragile, she tilted the notebook toward Mikki.

Mikki's eyes widened as she scanned the page. She flipped to the next one. Then another. Her movements were careful, like she knew she was being trusted with something important.

"Yo," Mikki whispered. "This is really good."

Toni froze. "You don't have to say that."

"I do," Mikki said, without hesitation. "Why isn't this a book already?"

Toni let out a nervous laugh. "Because it's just... stuff."

"Stuff that's amazing," Mikki said. "You make whole worlds."

The words settled into Toni's chest and stayed there.

She did not know how to respond. She only knew that something had shifted, something small but permanent. Like a door had cracked open and light had slipped in before she could stop it.

That moment followed her.

It followed her into Grandma Dot's backyard, where the notebook no longer felt like a shield she hid behind, but a tool she carried with purpose. When Mikki handed her the clipboard and asked her to sketch the platform, Toni's hands shook just a little before she began.

"You see things we don't," Mikki had said. "You imagine before the rest of us even believe."

Now, sitting beneath the trees with the sounds of summer buzzing around them, Toni understood what that meant.

For the first time, someone had not asked her to be quieter.

They had asked her to be seen.

After that day, the notebook stopped feeling like something Toni hid.

It still lived pressed against her chest, still rode everywhere with her, but now it had a different weight. Not heavier exactly. More intentional. Like it had a job to do.

In Grandma Dot's backyard, Toni found herself opening it without being asked. She sketched while Mikki talked through measurements, her pencil moving in quick, confident strokes. She wrote down Zee's quiet observations in the margins, little notes circled and underlined twice. She captured Jayda mid motion, arms thrown wide, braids flying behind her like punctuation marks at the end of a sentence.

Sometimes she did not even realize she was writing until her hand cramped.

The notebook had become a bridge.

When Zee leaned over her shoulder and pointed to a corner of the page, Toni adjusted the drawing without hesitation.

"If we loop it here," Zee said, voice low, "we can bring the harness back up without climbing every time."

Toni nodded and erased a line, redrawing it cleaner, sharper. "Like this."

Zee's eyes lit up. "Exactly."

Jayda squinted at the page. "Why do we look like superheroes in this sketch."

Toni felt her face heat. "It's just how I picture it."

Jayda grinned. "I like how you picture things."

That simple sentence stayed with her.

Nobody laughed. Nobody teased her for adding flair, for imagining more than what was strictly necessary. The notebook passed between them, resting in different hands, but always finding its way back to Toni like it knew where it belonged.

For the first time, her words were not something she had to protect.

They were something people used.

Later, after the yard emptied and the shadows stretched long, Toni sat on her bed with the notebook open to a fresh page. The room smelled faintly of clean laundry and the strawberry lotion she used on her hands. Outside, the sky softened from blue to lavender, the first stars blinking into view.

She stared at the blank page longer than usual.

Then she wrote.

Not a story this time. Not a castle or a moon girl or a mystery waiting to be solved.

Just the truth.

One day, I'll write about us.

The words looked strange and powerful sitting there alone. She added more beneath them, slower now, choosing carefully.

Four girls. One summer. Something we built together.

She paused, pencil hovering, then kept going.

Not because we were fearless.

Not because we got everything right.

But because we tried.

Toni leaned back against her pillow, the notebook resting on her chest, the pencil slipping from her fingers. Her heart felt full in a way she did not have language for yet.

She did not know how the story would end.

She did not know what would go wrong.

All she knew was that she was no longer writing from the outside.

She was inside the story now.

Chapter 5
The Sleepover Pact

The sun slid down behind the trees slowly, like it was reluctant to leave.

Orange and purple stretched across the sky in wide, uneven strokes, the colors bleeding into one another until the whole neighborhood looked softened around the edges. The heat of the day lingered, heavy but less sharp now, like it had finally decided to loosen its grip. Crickets had already begun their nightly chorus, loud and steady, the sound rising from the grass and settling into the spaces between breaths. Somewhere close by, a screen door slapped shut. Somewhere farther away, a car passed, its tires humming briefly before the noise faded back into summer quiet.

Inside Grandma Dot's house, the windows were open just enough to let the evening in.

The air smelled sweet, thick with honeysuckle drifting in from the yard and the faint buttery warmth of cornbread cooling on the counter. The scent clung to the room, wrapping itself around everything, familiar and grounding. The kind of smell that made you feel like you had arrived somewhere safe, even if you did not know why.

The living room no longer looked like a living room.

It had been transformed into something softer, braver.

Sleeping bags covered the floor in a loose, uneven circle, their colors clashing and overlapping. Pillows were stacked into lopsided walls, some flat and worn, others overstuffed and sagging at the seams. Quilts draped over the backs of chairs and the couch, patchworked galaxies stitched together by hands that had worked slowly and patiently for decades. Each square carried its own history, its own memory, sewn into place without asking permission.

A battery powered lantern glowed in the center of the room, its light warm and unsteady. It pulsed faintly, like a heartbeat that had not decided yet whether it was excited or afraid. Shadows danced along the walls, stretching and shrinking with every small movement.

The house itself seemed to watch.

The honey-colored walls were lined with framed photographs, sepia toned smiles frozen in time. Weddings. Graduations. Babies held carefully in tired arms. Eyes followed the room in quiet witness, as if the past was leaning in to see what the present was becoming. The bookshelves leaned just slightly to one side, filled with everything from thick dictionaries to folded church programs and paperbacks with cracked spines. The floor creaked near the hallway, the same spot it always had, like it was clearing its throat before speaking.

Everything felt slower here.

Time stretched itself thin and gentle, settling in beside them without rushing. The night had not fully arrived yet, but it was close enough to feel. The kind of night that invited secrets. The kind that made it easier to say things you usually kept tucked away.

Outside, the crickets grew louder, their buzzing swelling and falling in waves. Inside, the lantern hummed softly. The house breathed around them, old and patient, holding space for whatever was about to be spoken.

This was not just a sleepover.

It felt like a pause.

A moment where the world stepped back just far enough for four girls to sit inside it together, wrapped in quilts and borrowed courage, unaware of how much this night would matter later.

For now, there was only the settling in.

Jayda claimed her spot immediately.

The beanbag chair sat in the corner like it had been waiting for her, oversized and red velvet with a tear along one seam that puffed out stuffing whenever someone leaned too hard against it. Jayda launched herself into it without hesitation, disappearing almost completely until only her knees and the swinging ends of her braids were visible. Glitter covered socks dangled over the edge, toes wiggling every time she laughed.

"This is mine," she announced, voice echoing slightly off the walls. "Anybody try to take it, we fighting."

No one argued.

Zee settled near the lantern on a crocheted blanket that smelled faintly of cedar and lavender. The blanket was made of mismatched squares, colors that should not have worked together but somehow did. Turquoise sat beside maroon. Lemon yellow pressed up against forest green. It looked like something built slowly, patiently, without worrying too much about rules. Zee knelt at one edge of it, pulling a length of purple rope from her backpack and beginning to braid it, fingers moving in a steady, practiced rhythm.

The rope slid through her hands like it belonged there.

Mikki leaned against the couch, stretching her legs out in front of her. The couch was faded floral with carved wooden legs and cushions that sighed softly under weight. One arm had a small tear Grandma Dot had covered with a lace doily years ago, like it was a secret only the house remembered. Mikki balanced her clipboard on a squishy green pillow with gold tassels on the corners, a faint coffee stain marking one edge from last Christmas. She flipped through pages slowly, pencil tapping against the plastic as if she was checking in with her own thoughts.

Toni sat cross legged on her sleeping bag, pale pink with a rip near the zipper. The notebook rested in her lap like a shield, familiar and solid. The word IMAGINE caught the lantern light in crooked silver letters, one rhinestone missing from the I. Her fingers traced the empty space absently, over and over, like she was waiting for it to grow back.

For a while, they talked about nothing.

School gossip. Summer shows they had half watched. The weird way time felt different at night, stretched thin and quiet. Popsicle wrappers crinkled as they ate, juice dripping down wrists and onto napkins. Jayda laughed too loud at something that was not that funny. Mikki shushed her automatically, then smiled when she realized there was no reason to be quiet. Zee listened more than she spoke, braid growing longer in her lap. Toni scribbled notes in the margins of her notebook, not stories yet, just observations she did not want to lose.

The circle settled.

Jayda shifted in the beanbag, kicking her feet lightly against the side. Zee adjusted her position on the blanket, knees tucked closer. Mikki leaned back on her elbows, staring up at the ceiling where shadows moved slowly. Toni pulled her sleeping bag tighter around her legs.

Without anyone saying it out loud, they had each chosen their place.

Not just in the room.

With each other.

The way Jayda took up space without apology. The way Zee anchored herself close to the center. The way Mikki hovered between planning and resting. The way Toni stayed just slightly guarded, notebook close, eyes open and observant.

It felt deliberate.

Like everyone had arrived carrying exactly what they were meant to bring.

The lantern flickered softly.

Outside, the night pressed closer to the windows.

Inside, four girls sat in a circle that was beginning to feel like something more than coincidence.

For a few minutes, no one spoke.

The lantern hummed quietly in the center of the room, its light pulsing faintly, casting shadows that stretched and shifted across the walls. The crickets outside kept up their steady chorus, loud enough to remind them the world was still moving, even if this room felt suspended in time. Somewhere in the house, a pipe clicked as it cooled, the sound sharp and brief before settling again.

Mikki was the one who broke the quiet.

"What are you scared of?" she asked.

Her voice was low, almost casual, like she was asking about favorite colors or summer plans. But the question landed differently. It settled into the space between them and stayed there.

Jayda stopped kicking her feet. Zee's hands froze mid braid, the rope caught halfway through a loop. Toni looked up from her notebook, pencil hovering just above the page.

Jayda snorted first, because that was her instinct. "What, like snakes?" she said, reaching blindly for the popcorn bowl beside her. "Because snakes are a hard no."

Mikki smiled, but she did not laugh. She did not look down at her clipboard either. She kept her eyes on the ceiling, like she was giving the question room to breathe.

"Not stuff like that," she said. "The real kind."

Jayda paused, popcorn halfway to her mouth. "Then what kind."

"The kind you don't joke about," Mikki said.

The lantern buzzed.

The air shifted.

Jayda sat up in the beanbag, the stuffing sighing beneath her as she moved. She picked at the loose thread near the tear, eyes locked on it like it might give her an answer if she stared long enough.

"I'm scared of quiet," she said finally.

No one laughed.

"Not the good quiet," she added quickly, voice flattening. "Not this. I mean the kind after yelling. When a door slams and nobody says anything. When the TV's off and the house feels too clean." She swallowed. "Like you're waiting for something bad to happen, and it already did, but nobody says it out loud."

The room stayed still.

Zee lowered her eyes, fingers tightening around the rope before she forced herself to keep braiding. Slower now. More careful.

"I know that quiet," she said softly.

She did not explain.

She did not have to.

Toni leaned forward, her notebook slipping slightly in her lap. "What happens in that kind of quiet?" she asked, voice gentle.

Jayda shrugged, but her shoulders were tense. "You shrink," she said. "You try not to make noise. You try not to take up space. Just in case."

Zee's braid slipped through her fingers, the rope warm from her hands. "I'm scared I'll mess something up," she said, barely above a whisper. "Like what if one of my knots slips. What if someone gets hurt because I thought I tied it right."

She stared at the rope in her lap like it might answer her.

Mikki sat up straighter, the clipboard sliding off the pillow and landing softly on the floor. "I think about that too," she admitted. "What if I measure wrong. What if I push too fast. What if I build something I can't fix."

The words trembled as they left her mouth, like she had been holding them in for a while.

Toni reached out without thinking and placed her notebook on the floor between them, open but blank, like an offering. "You're the most careful person I know," she said to Zee. "If anyone can make a knot that holds, it's you."

Zee's lips twitched, just slightly.

Jayda flicked the end of the braid with her finger. "And if it doesn't," she said, lighter now but not careless, "that's what I'm here for. I crash. I bounce. I get back up."

They laughed then.

Not loudly.

Not the kind of laugh that filled space.

The kind that loosened something tight inside all of them at once.

Mikki picked up her clipboard again, staring at the blue marker lines like they suddenly felt fragile. "I'm scared I'm not enough," she said quietly. "That I'll build something too big and won't know how to stop it."

Zee reached into her backpack and pulled out a small roll of medical tape, still sealed. She placed it gently in Mikki's palm.

"Just in case," she said.

The lantern flickered.

Outside, the night leaned closer to the house, listening.

Inside, the girls stayed where they were, fear named and shared, no longer heavy enough to pull them apart.

The lantern burned a little lower as the night stretched on.

Its glow shifted from bright white to something warmer, softer, turning the room amber and rose. Shadows leaned against the walls and pooled beneath the furniture. Outside, the wind brushed the lace curtains, lifting them just enough to let cool air slip inside. Somewhere far off, thunder rumbled once, low and distant, like the sky clearing its throat and deciding to stay quiet for now.

They rearranged themselves without really thinking about it.

Jayda stretched out across the floor, one arm flung dramatically over her eyes, the beanbag finally abandoned. Zee curled onto her side on the crocheted blanket, the rope still resting near her hands like she wasn't quite ready to let it go. Mikki propped herself on one elbow, chewing lightly on the end of her pencil, eyes fixed on the blueprint as if the lines might rearrange themselves while she watched. Toni stayed sitting up, legs crossed, notebook trembling just slightly in her hands.

"I wrote something," Toni said.

Her voice was so quiet at first that Jayda peeked out from behind her arm to make sure she had heard right.

"It's not finished," Toni added quickly. "I just... I think I want to read it."

No one rushed her.

No one joked.

They turned toward her slowly, like they didn't want to scare the moment away.

Toni swallowed and flipped to a folded page near the back of her notebook. The lantern light caught the glitter stickers on the cover, scattering faint reflections across her hands. She cleared her throat once, then read.

"We are the girls who leap first.
Who dream loud, build high, and dare the wind to hold us.
We are the ones who carry tape in our pockets
And blueprints in our hearts.
We are the ones who fall
And still fly."

When she finished, the room stayed quiet.

But it was a different quiet than before.

Not heavy.

Not sharp.

Whole.

Mikki was the first to move. She reached for a blue marker from the pile of supplies near her sleeping bag, clicking the cap off with purpose. "We should sign it," she said. "For real."

Toni blinked. "Sign it?"

"Yeah," Mikki said, already sliding the notebook closer. "Like a pact."

Jayda pushed herself upright immediately. "I call first."

She grabbed the marker and wrote big and looping across the bottom of the page, the letters bold and unapologetic.

Crash Queen.

Zee took the marker next. Her handwriting was smaller, steadier, each letter careful and deliberate.

Zahara-Anchor.

Toni hesitated for just a second before adding her name, the pencil dents from earlier pages guiding her hand.

Toni B.-Storyteller.

Mikki signed last, pressing the marker harder than necessary, her letters strong but slightly uneven.

Mikkaela-Builder.

They stared at the page together.

Four names.

One sheet of paper.

Something settled between them, quiet and certain.

Their hands stacked in the middle without anyone suggesting it. Warm palms. Slight trembles. Real contact that grounded them all at once.

"Tomorrow," Mikki whispered into the dim room, her voice steadier now, "we start building the thing that'll carry us into the sky."

No one argued.

No one laughed.

They lay back down after that, the sleeping bags rustling softly as they shifted into more comfortable positions. The lantern dimmed further, its glow barely enough to outline their shapes. Breathing slowed. Thoughts drifted.

Outside, the night listened.

And waited.

The lantern finally clicked to its lowest setting, a soft amber glow barely bright enough to trace the edges of the room. The living room breathed the way old houses do at night, slow and familiar. A floorboard sighed near the hallway. The bookshelf leaned into its shadows. The quilts shifted as the girls settled, fabric whispering against fabric.

Jayda was the first to break the quiet, but she kept her voice low this time. "If we die tomorrow," she said, "I want it on record that I picked the good sleeping spot."

Mikki snorted softly into her pillow. "Nobody is dying tomorrow."

"That's what people always say the day before they become legends," Jayda replied.

Zee turned her head slightly, braid pressed against her cheek. "You are not a legend," she said. "You are dramatic."

Jayda grinned in the dark. "Same thing."

Toni smiled without lifting her head. She had set her notebook on the floor beside her sleeping bag, closed now, like it had said everything it needed to for the night. Her fingers rested on the cover anyway, tracing the raised letters of IMAGINE as if they might warm under her touch.

The quiet returned, gentler this time.

Outside, the crickets resumed their chorus, steady and patient. Somewhere down the block, a screen door creaked shut. A car passed, tires humming against pavement before the sound faded away. The world went on, unaware of the promise that had just been made on a living room floor.

Mikki stared at the ceiling, counting the tiny cracks in the paint she had never noticed before. Her mind ran ahead, as it always did. Measurements. Angles. Tomorrow. She forced herself to slow down, matching her breathing to the soft rhythm of the room.

Zee lay still, listening. She counted sounds instead of breaths. Crickets. Wind in the trees. The faint tick of the lantern cooling. Her hands rested open now, no rope between them, and that felt like a decision she was still learning how to make.

Jayda stretched, then stilled, her usual restlessness quieted for once. The day replayed behind her eyes. The laughter. The words spoken without jokes wrapped around them. The way nobody had told her to lower her voice or calm down. Her chest felt warm, like something had finally settled where it belonged.

Toni shifted onto her side, facing the center of the room. She thought about the names on the page. How strange and perfect it felt to see them together. Not characters. Not ideas. Real people. Real voices. A real story she was standing inside instead of watching from the edge.

"I'm glad we did this," she whispered.

No one answered right away.

Then Mikki said softly, "Me too."

Zee nodded in the dark. Jayda hummed once, a low sound of agreement.

Sleep came slowly, the way it always does when something important has been said. It crept in around the edges, gentle and patient, until breathing evened out and thoughts loosened their grip.

By the time the lantern finally went dark, the promise was already woven into them.

Tomorrow waited.

But for now, they rested.

Chapter 6
The Trouble with Rope

The next morning smelled like rain that had already decided it was finished with the day before.

The grass in Grandma Dot's backyard was still damp, cool beneath their sneakers, each step darkening the soil just a shade more. Moisture clung to everything, to hems of shorts and loose curls and the edges of notebooks tucked under arms. The air felt close, heavy without being hot yet, the kind of morning that pressed against skin and made you aware of every breath you took. Above them, clouds thinned and shifted slowly, letting pale sunlight slip through in uneven patches.

When the light hit just right, droplets still clinging to the clothesline bent into tiny flashes of color. Brief. Fragile. Gone almost as soon as you noticed them.

Mikki stood near the center of the yard, clipboard hugged tight against her chest, eyes lifted toward the trees.

They had chosen them carefully.

The oak on the left was wide and steady, its trunk thick enough that three people linking arms could not wrap all the way around it. A jagged scar ran down one side where lightning had struck years ago, the bark darker there, rougher. Grandma Dot liked to tell that story whenever she noticed someone staring too long. How the tree had split with a sound like thunder inside thunder. How it had survived anyway.

The tree on the right was slimmer, its trunk bent slightly toward the fence, as if it had spent its whole life leaning into wind that never quite stopped. Its branches reached outward, stubborn and angled, leaves whispering softly whenever the air shifted.

Together, they framed the yard like sentinels. Old. Watching. Unmoved by excitement or fear.

"We've got about forty feet between them," Mikki said, mostly to herself. She flipped the clipboard around and scanned her notes, pencil tapping once, then stopping. "That gives us the height we need, but the angle has to be right. Too steep and the speed's wrong. Too shallow and you lose momentum."

She exhaled slowly.

Yesterday, those numbers had felt thrilling. Full of possibility.

Today, they felt heavy.

Jayda sat on the porch steps, tying and retying her sneaker like she was killing time on purpose. The beads in her braids were quieter than usual, dulled by the damp air. "You really woke up choosing math," she said. "Couldn't be me."

Mikki smiled faintly but did not look away from the trees. "You'll appreciate it when you don't slam into the shed."

Jayda grinned. "I like a little drama."

Zee stood nearby, ladder already dragged into position, rope slung over her shoulder. She watched Mikki's face closely, reading it the way she read tension in knots and fibers. Something had shifted since last night. The promise was still there, warm and real, but now it carried weight.

Responsibility.

Toni hovered at the edge of the yard, notebook tucked against her side, watching all of them. She noticed how Mikki kept checking the same measurement twice. How Jayda's jokes landed softer. How Zee's grip on the rope tightened just a little before she even climbed.

The pact from the night before had not faded with sleep.

It had settled.

Mikki lowered her clipboard and finally nodded to herself. "Okay," she said. "We start slow."

No one argued.

The morning felt like a pause held on purpose. A breath taken before movement. Not fear exactly. Something closer to respect.

Above them, the trees did not shift. They waited.

And for the first time since the idea had been born, all four girls understood that building something meant listening just as much as leaping.

They moved with more intention than they had the day before.

Zee climbed the ladder first, testing each rung with her foot before trusting it with her weight. The wood creaked softly under her, a sound that made Jayda glance up from the steps and pause mid joke. Zee did not rush. She never did. The rope rested over her shoulder, thick and coiled, the fibers still stiff and clean. When she reached the branch, she stopped and pressed her palm flat against the bark, grounding herself the way she always did before tying anything that mattered.

Below her, Mikki paced the distance between the trees again, counting steps under her breath. She checked the clipboard, then the ground, then the angle of the ladder. Her pencil hovered, hesitated, then scribbled a small correction in the margin. It was not a big change. Barely noticeable. But it made her shoulders relax just a little.

Toni knelt beside the open toolbox, sorting with quiet focus. Bolts went into one neat pile. Carabiners into another. She lined them up by size without realizing she was doing it, the way her mind always organized stories before she ever wrote a first sentence. Her notebook lay open beside her, a new page waiting. At the top, she wrote carefully, Flight Sketches, Attempt One, then underlined it twice.

Jayda drifted closer, hands shoved into her pockets, eyes tracking Zee's movements above. "You sure you don't want help up there?" she called.

Zee shook her head without looking down. "I've got it."

Jayda shrugged and grabbed the base of the ladder anyway, planting her feet wide and steadying it with both hands. "Just in case," she said, echoing Zee's favorite phrase with a grin.

Zee threaded the rope around the branch slowly, letting it slide through her fingers as she measured by feel as much as sight. She tied the first knot, then paused. Tugged once. Twice. The rope dipped, then settled. She adjusted the knot and tied it again, tighter this time, her fingers moving with practiced certainty.

"Test it," Mikki called.

Zee leaned back and put her weight into it. The rope held. Leaves rustled. The branch shifted slightly, then stilled.

"Again," Mikki said.

Zee tested it again, harder. Still solid.

Toni looked up from her notebook. "I'm writing down how many times we test," she said. "So we don't forget later."

Mikki nodded. "Good."

Jayda laughed softly. "We really out here doing this like a science fair."

"No," Mikki said. "Better."

They worked like that for a while. Adjusting. Measuring. Writing. Laughing when the ladder scraped too loudly against the bark or when Jayda pretended to narrate like a sports announcer. The rhythm felt careful but not tense. Focused without being stiff.

For a moment, the yard felt right again.

Then Zee climbed down, wiping her palms on her jeans, and glanced at the remaining coil of rope on the ground. Her eyes narrowed just slightly.

"This section looks thinner," she said.

Mikki stepped closer, crouching beside her. She ran her fingers along the fibers, feeling the subtle change Zee had noticed immediately.

"It's worn," Mikki said quietly. "Probably from before."

Jayda leaned in. "Is that bad bad, or just replace it later bad."

Zee did not answer right away. She traced the frayed spot once more, slow and thoughtful.

"It means we don't ignore it," she said.

The air shifted again. Not fear. Awareness.

Toni wrote that down too.

The voice came from the other side of the fence.

"Y'all better not be trying to fly out here."

Jayda groaned before anyone even turned around. "Please tell me that is not who I think it is."

Malik leaned over the wooden slats like he had been there the whole time, arms folded across his chest, a basketball tucked against his hip. His sunglasses were pushed up onto his head, catching the pale morning light. He wore the same grin he always did when he knew he was about to get a reaction.

"This is wild," he continued, eyes flicking from the ladder to the rope to Mikki's clipboard. "Ropes in trees? Backyard engineering? That's how you end up on the evening news."

Jayda rolled her eyes hard. "Go away, Malik."

He laughed like she had just proved his point. "I'm serious. 'Local kids attempt stunt, regret everything.' I can see the headline now."

Mikki straightened, clipboard pressed tighter against her chest. "We're being careful," she said. "We measured everything."

Malik raised an eyebrow. "Oh cool. Did your calculator tell you gravity took the day off too?"

The words landed heavier than the joke was meant to carry.

Zee climbed down one rung on the ladder, wiping her palms on her jeans. "We're not just playing," she said, her voice steady but firm.

Malik's gaze shifted to her, then back to the rope stretched between the trees. For a second, the grin slipped. "I'm just saying," he said, shrugging. "That thing snaps, somebody's gonna get hurt."

He bounced the basketball once against the concrete, the sound sharp and hollow in the quiet yard. Then he turned and walked off, whistling like he had not just dropped a shadow across their morning.

The fence creaked softly as it settled back into place.

For a moment, no one spoke.

Jayda kicked at a clump of damp dirt, breaking the silence. "He's just trying to scare us. Ignore him."

Mikki did not answer.

Her eyes stayed on the rope. On the knot Zee had tied. On the way it rested against the branch like it belonged there. Malik's words echoed anyway, unwelcome and insistent.

What if he's right.

She swallowed. "What if we're rushing this," she said quietly.

Zee looked at her, really looked this time. "We tested the tension."

"Once," Mikki said. "We tested it once."

Toni stood, brushing dirt from her knees. "We can test it again," she said quickly. "Or add a backup. Write down everything. Do it slower."

Jayda crossed her arms, the joking edge gone from her face. "I don't like him being right about anything," she said. "But... yeah. Slower."

The doubt did not undo the work they had done.

But it seeped in anyway.

And the rope felt heavier for it.

They moved more carefully after that.

Zee climbed the ladder again, slower this time, testing each rung before trusting it with her weight. Mikki paced beneath her, eyes darting between the rope and the numbers on her clipboard, recalculating angles she had already calculated twice. Toni knelt near the toolbox, reorganizing bolts and clamps that had already been sorted, her pencil tapping a nervous rhythm against the page. Even Jayda was quieter than usual, watching instead of talking, hands shoved deep into her pockets.

"Let's run a stress check," Mikki said finally. "Not just tension. Load."

Zee nodded. "I'll loop it through again."

She fed the rope through the pulley, fingers working with practiced precision. The fibers slid through smoothly at first, rough but cooperative. Zee leaned back slightly, putting her weight into it, watching how the line responded.

It dipped.

Not much. Just enough.

"Hold up," Mikki said.

Zee froze.

Before anyone could say anything else, a sharp sound cracked through the air.

Snap.

It was quick and loud and wrong.

A short length of rope whipped sideways, slapping hard against the side of the shed with a flat, angry sound. The pulley jerked. The remaining line shuddered, then went still.

Everyone jumped.

For a split second, the yard felt too quiet, like the world itself had stopped to see what they would do next.

Jayda was the first to move. She crouched and picked up the loose end of rope, turning it over in her hands. The fibers were frayed and uneven, not cleanly cut, like they had given up instead of breaking outright.

"That's not supposed to happen," she said, her voice lower than usual.

Mikki's clipboard slipped from her fingers and landed in the grass with a dull thud. Her chest felt tight, like the air had thickened around her ribs.

"This is stupid," she muttered. "We're not ready."

Toni shook her head immediately. "No. That rope was old. We can replace it. We can—"

"Or maybe this was a dumb idea," Jayda said, standing. "We're out here acting like engineers, but we're just kids."

Zee climbed down the ladder and sat heavily in the grass. Her braid slipped over her shoulder as she dropped her gaze to her hands. Her fingers curled inward, nails pressing into her palms.

"I didn't expect it to fray like that," she said quietly. "I should have checked the age of the rope."

Mikki lowered herself beside her, knees pulled tight to her chest. Her eyes burned, but she kept her face steady. "I thought I planned for everything. We had a blueprint. We talked about angles and knots."

"We didn't test stress under load," Zee said. "That's on me."

Toni knelt between them, her notebook pressed flat against the grass like an anchor. "It's not on you. It's a problem. And problems can be solved."

Jayda dropped backward onto the damp grass, staring up at the clouds. "Do you think real engineers feel like this," she asked, "when stuff breaks and everybody looks at each other like maybe they messed up?"

"Yes," Mikki said without hesitation. "All the time."

Jayda huffed. "Good. I'd hate to think we're the only ones."

They stayed like that for a while. No one rushing to fix anything. No one pretending it was fine. The excitement from the morning had drained away, replaced by something heavier but also more honest.

Then Zee sat up.

She brushed grass from her jeans and reached into her backpack. When she pulled her hand out, she was holding a coil of rope so bright it almost didn't belong in the muted yard. Thick. New. Yellow as sunlight.

"I brought backup," she said.

Mikki stared at it. "You did."

Zee nodded once. "Just in case."

Jayda sat up and grinned, relief breaking through her seriousness. "And that," she said, "is why you're the anchor."

Toni uncapped her marker and wrote carefully at the top of a fresh page.

Flight Sketches

Trial Two

Mikki stood, a deep breath settling her shoulders back into place. "Okay," she said. "We start over. Slower. Smarter."

They did not rush.

They rebuilt.

Starting over felt different than starting the first time.

The air had warmed slightly, the dampness lifting off the grass in thin, ghostlike wisps as the sun pushed higher through the clouds. Birds had returned to the trees, chirping cautiously, like they were checking to see if the danger had passed. Somewhere down the street, a screen door slammed and a radio crackled to life, the ordinary sounds of the neighborhood easing back into place.

Zee laid the new rope out carefully, straightening it along the ground so it wouldn't twist. She ran the length of it through her hands, feeling for weak spots, tugging gently, then harder. The rope didn't complain. It held.

"This one's rated for way more than we need," she said, mostly to reassure herself.

Mikki nodded, scribbling notes onto her clipboard. She had added a new column labeled Failure Points, the words underlined twice. "We double anchor," she said. "And we don't skip any tests. Even the boring ones."

Jayda stretched her arms overhead and rolled her shoulders. "I officially hate boring," she said. "But I hate falling more."

Toni smiled faintly and wrote that down too.

They worked in layers now. Nothing happened just once. Every knot was tied, checked, untied, and tied again. Every measurement was taken, called out, written down, and verified. When Zee climbed the ladder again, Jayda stood at the base, one hand braced against the side, steady and alert. When Mikki adjusted the angle, Toni read the numbers back to her, slow and precise.

No one joked about shortcuts.

At one point, Mikki stepped back and frowned at the setup, her pencil hovering over the clipboard. "This feels... different," she said.

Jayda tilted her head. "Different bad or different smarter."

"Different smarter," Mikki decided. "Like we actually learned something."

Zee tightened the final knot and leaned back, testing the rope with her full weight. It dipped smoothly, then settled, solid and sure.

She exhaled.

"Okay," she said. "That's better."

They didn't test it with a jump yet. Nobody suggested it. Instead, they loaded the line with a heavy bucket filled with rocks, lifting it inch by inch, watching how the rope responded. The pulley groaned slightly, then smoothed out.

It held.

Mikki's shoulders loosened for the first time all day. "Tomorrow," she said. "We test again. With a person."

Jayda grinned. "You know that's me."

"We'll see," Mikki said, but she was smiling too.

As they packed up for the afternoon, Zee coiled the leftover rope carefully and tucked it back into her bag. Her fingers brushed the edge of her jar, the familiar clink of metal inside grounding her.

Not everything broke because you were careless, she thought. Sometimes things broke because you hadn't learned enough yet.

That didn't mean you quit.

It meant you paid attention.

As they left the yard, the rope stayed behind, stretched neatly between the trees, brighter than before, steadier too. It didn't look finished yet.

But it looked like something worth trusting.

And that, they were beginning to understand, was its own kind of progress.

Chapter 7
Operation Zipline

By the time the sun climbed high enough to sit directly overhead, the girls were already tired.

Not the kind of tired that came from boredom, but the deep, satisfying ache that settled into muscles after hours of real work. Their hands were sticky with sap and rope fibers, palms rubbed raw in places where the skin had not yet toughened. Dirt streaked their legs and knees. Sweat clung to their backs and gathered at their hairlines, making curls and braids stick where they touched skin.

None of them complained.

The tiredness did not hit all at once. It came in layers.

It settled first in their hands. Fingers stiff from gripping rope too long. Palms sore where fibers had rubbed the skin raw despite the tape. Zee flexed her hands slowly, feeling the pull beneath her knuckles, the faint sting that reminded her how many times she had tied the same knots over and over again. Each knot felt slightly different. Each one demanded attention. She welcomed the ache. It meant she had not rushed.

Mikki felt it in her shoulders. The dull burn that came from climbing up and down the ladder too many times, from holding the clipboard tucked tight against her body like letting it go might cause the whole plan to scatter. Sweat slid down her spine and disappeared into the waistband of her shorts. She barely noticed anymore. Numbers still lined up in her head. Angles. Distances. Weight. She rolled her shoulders once and adjusted her stance, grounding herself before checking the rig again.

Toni noticed the fatigue in smaller ways. The way her pencil pressed harder into the page without her realizing it. The way her handwriting slanted when her wrist grew tired. She shook out her hand and switched grips, pausing only long enough to drink from her water bottle before going back to her notes. The page mattered. Capturing this mattered. If she stopped writing, it felt like something important might slip past unseen.

Jayda felt the exhaustion everywhere at once. In her calves from pacing. In her lower back from standing too long without realizing she needed to sit. In the tightness behind her eyes from squinting into the sun. She cracked her neck once, then again, rolling her shoulders with exaggerated drama that earned no reaction from the others. That was how she knew it was real work. Nobody had energy left to laugh at her.

The sun climbed higher.

It pressed straight down now, no longer angled or forgiving. Shade shrank beneath the trees, retreating inch by inch as the morning slid toward afternoon. The air thickened, wrapping itself around them like damp fabric. Sweat dried and reappeared in cycles, leaving salt behind on skin and rope alike. Even the birds quieted for stretches at a time, as if they too were conserving energy.

Still, no one suggested stopping.

Breaks happened quietly. A shared water bottle passed from hand to hand. A moment leaning against the trunk of The Lookout, back pressed to bark warm from the sun. A few slow breaths taken deliberately before climbing again. These pauses were not quitting. They were part of the work.

What surprised Toni most was how natural it felt.

No one complained. No one counted the hours out loud. No one asked how much longer they had to do this. The tiredness bonded them in a way excitement never could. It made every movement intentional. Every decision heavier, and therefore more important.

This was not play.

This was choosing to stay.

The trees stood tall above them, unmoving and watchful. Over the past few days, they had started giving them names without even realizing it. The thicker oak on the left was The Lookout, wide and steady, its branches spreading like arms meant to hold. The slimmer tree on the right, bent just slightly toward the yard, was The Launch Tree. It was the one they would climb. The one that would give them lift.

Mikki wiped her forehead with the back of her wrist and stepped onto the ladder, clipboard tucked under one arm. The ladder creaked in protest, but she trusted it. She always tested the things she climbed.

"Zee," she called up toward the branch. "You doubled the anchor knot on this side, right?"

Zee stood below, feet planted firmly in the grass, one hand gripping the rope. Her fingers were wrapped in sports tape now, the white strips crisscrossing her skin where blisters had formed from days of tying and retying.

"Doubled and tested," Zee said. "Three times."

Mikki nodded. "Okay. Let's finish the pulley rig."

Jayda strutted over holding the harness, swinging it casually at her side. "So are we testing this with a backpack first," she asked, "or are we letting me fly."

"Backpack first," Toni said immediately from where she stood beneath the trees. "One hundred percent backpack first."

She had arranged a pile of books inside an old canvas tote bag, tying the top securely with twine. In bold marker across the front, she had written Flight Dummy One and drawn a lopsided smiley face beneath it.

Jayda eyed it skeptically. "That thing looks like it's judging me."

"That's because it knows what you're about to do," Toni replied.

Mikki laughed softly. "No danger," she said, more to reassure herself than anyone else.

Zee clipped the bag into the harness carefully, checking the connection twice before lifting it off the ground. The rope dipped slightly under the weight, then steadied. She guided it up the line, eyes tracking every inch as it moved.

The pulley squeaked.

Everyone froze.

Zee stopped immediately, holding the rope still. She waited, listening. The squeak did not come again.

She eased the bag forward.

It slid smoothly this time, gliding down the line faster than any of them expected. The tote zipped across the yard and dropped neatly into the pile of hay they had dragged from the shed, landing with a soft thump and a puff of yellow dust.

"Yes," Mikki whispered, breathless.

Jayda clapped once, loud and sharp. "Now that's what I'm talking about."

They worked through the heat, the hours blurring together.

Time stopped behaving normally.

It did not move in neat lines anymore. It stretched and folded, broke into pieces that felt both endless and gone too quickly. The sun climbed, stalled, shifted just enough to remind them it was still there. Shadows crawled across the yard, inching forward while no one paid them any attention.

Zee lost track of how many times she had tied and untied the same knot.

Her fingers ached in a dull, familiar way, the kind of pain that told her she was doing something worth finishing. She tested tension by feel now, not just sight. A pull too sharp meant trouble later. A give too soft meant the knot was lying. She listened to the rope the way other people listened to voices, attentive to the smallest change.

She adjusted without being asked.

A half turn here. A retie there. Tape added where fibers rubbed too closely against bark or metal. When she paused, it was not from doubt. It was from patience.

Mikki watched everything.

She paced, measured, stopped, recalculated, then did it again. Numbers crowded her mind, but they did not overwhelm her. They lined up, waiting to be checked, waiting to be proven right. She erased clean lines and replaced them with darker ones, pressing harder each time like certainty could be transferred through graphite.

She timed each test run, clicking her stopwatch the second the pulley moved, stopping it the moment the load landed. She wrote the times down twice, once in ink and once in pencil, as if the redundancy mattered.

It did.

Every successful run loosened her shoulders a fraction. Every hesitation tightened them again.

Toni drifted between them, the quiet constant.

She documented everything. Angles. Adjustments. Jokes that felt important enough to remember. The way Zee paused before retesting. The way Mikki stared at the line before changing anything. The way Jayda paced like movement itself was part of the build.

Her sketches grew more confident as the hours passed. Lines sharpened. Labels multiplied. Arrows pointed to improvements that had not been made yet but would be. The page filled, then another, then another. She was not just recording what was happening. She was mapping what could happen next.

Jayda refused to sit still.

She paced the perimeter of the yard, stepping over rope coils, circling the trees like a coach watching warmups. She narrated imaginary disasters and dramatic victories, voice booming and playful, but she never touched anything without permission.

Every time Zee tied, Jayda watched. Every time Mikki adjusted, Jayda listened.

She cracked jokes because silence made her nervous.

But she stayed close because leaving felt wrong.

At one point, the pulley hesitated just long enough to make Toni's pencil pause mid stroke.

Everyone froze again.

Zee tested the line. Mikki checked alignment. Jayda held her breath without realizing it.

Then the pulley smoothed out, the moment passing like a ripple across water.

Jayda exhaled loud enough to be dramatic. "Okkaaaaay," she said. "I don't like when it does that."

Mikki nodded. "Me neither."

So they adjusted.

Again.

The yard smelled like hot metal and crushed grass. Sweat soaked through collars and darkened the fabric at their backs. Hands brushed accidentally and pulled away just as fast, not from discomfort but from focus. Nobody complained. Nobody suggested stopping.

Work had a rhythm now.

Tie. Test. Adjust. Record. Repeat.

By the time the sun edged past its highest point, the system felt less fragile. Not invincible. Just honest. It responded the way it was supposed to. It behaved when treated correctly.

That mattered more than speed.

They were not rushing toward flight.

They were building something that deserved to last.

Zee reinforced every knot, fingers moving methodically, testing tension, adjusting angles. She paused often, listening to the rope, feeling it respond beneath her hands.

Mikki made small edits to the blueprint, erasing and redrawing, checking measurements again and again. She timed the test runs, scribbling notes in the margins, calculating speed and distance down to the inch.

Toni moved between them, recording updates in her notebook, sketching the setup from different angles. Her hands flew across the page, words and pictures spilling out like she was trying to capture something alive before it escaped.

Jayda paced the yard like a coach on game day, cracking jokes to keep the energy up. She mimed dramatic falls, narrated imaginary highlight reels, and declared herself the world's greatest stuntwoman.

Then she stopped.

She stood still beneath the line, head tipped back, eyes following the rope from one tree to the other. The jokes drained from her face, leaving something quieter behind.

"You think it'll hold me," she asked.

Her voice was softer than usual.

The question hung in the air, heavier than any of them expected.

Zee met her eyes without hesitation. "Yes."

Mikki nodded. "But we're making you a secondary harness. Just in case."

Jayda took a slow breath. "Okay."

They took turns testing the setup again.

They did not rush the order.

No one said it out loud, but they all understood why Zee went first.

She checked the harness on herself the same way she checked everything else. Fingers slid along straps, buckles tugged twice, then a third time just to be sure. She clipped in slowly, listening for the click, waiting for the sound to settle in her chest before trusting it.

"This is just a feel test," Mikki reminded her. "Not distance."

Zee nodded. "I know."

She stepped onto the platform and paused, one hand resting lightly on the rope. She did not jump. She leaned.

The line responded immediately, dipping just enough to acknowledge her weight before holding steady. Zee slid a short distance, feet skimming the air, body angled carefully as she tested balance, friction, response.

Her fingers tightened once.

Then relaxed.

She dropped into the hay below and stood up right away, scanning the line like it might surprise her if she looked away too long.

"Good," she said. Not relieved. Just certain.

Toni went next, even though no one expected her to volunteer.

She swallowed hard before climbing the ladder, laughing under her breath like she was trying to convince herself this was funny. Her hands shook as she clipped in, but she did not stop. She took her time, copying Zee's movements, listening to every sound the rope made.

"Just a little," Mikki said gently. "You don't have to go far."

"I know," Toni said. "I just want to feel it."

She stepped off.

The sensation stole a sound from her throat, half squeal, half gasp. She slid farther than she meant to, momentum carrying her just long enough to make her panic flare.

Then the rope held.

The hay caught her cleanly, soft and forgiving. Toni sat up laughing so hard it surprised her.

"I did it," she said, breathless. "I actually did it."

Jayda clapped once, loud and proud. "Storyteller flies!"

Mikki smiled, but she was already watching the rope again.

She tested last.

Carefully. Methodically. She clipped in, paused, then leaned back just enough to test resistance. She stopped herself partway down, hanging there for a moment as she studied the line, the angle, the way the pulley behaved under controlled load.

"Speed's consistent," she called. "No drag."

She slid the rest of the way down and landed, immediately reaching for her clipboard.

Another note. Another checkmark.

Another quiet yes.

Jayda waited.

She had been ready since the beginning, but now readiness felt different. Heavier. More deliberate. This was not just thrill anymore. This was trust.

She climbed the platform slowly, helmet strapped tight, harness snug across her shoulders. From the top, the yard looked smaller than she remembered. The trees leaned inward, close enough to feel like witnesses.

She glanced down once.

Then she didn't look again.

The girls met her eyes instead.

Zee's hands were steady on the rope. Toni's breath was caught somewhere between excitement and fear. Mikki's focus was razor sharp, eyes tracking every inch of line like nothing else existed.

They were not cheering.

They were holding her.

That mattered.

Zee clipped herself in first, sliding just a few feet to feel the balance. She adjusted the harness and climbed back down, nodding once.

Toni went next, climbing the platform with a nervous laugh. Her hands shook as she gripped the line, but she did not back down. She slid a short distance, squealing, then dropped safely into the hay below, laughing harder than before.

Mikki tested last, careful and controlled, stopping herself partway down to check tension and speed. She landed and immediately reached for her clipboard, jotting down another note.

Finally, it was Jayda's turn.

She stood at the top of the platform, harness secured, helmet strapped on tight. From up there, the yard looked smaller. The trees leaned closer. The ground felt farther away than it had before.

She glanced down.

Then she looked back at the girls.

They were not teasing now. Not joking. Zee stood with the rope gripped firmly in both hands. Toni held her breath, notebook forgotten at her side. Mikki watched the line, eyes sharp and focused.

They were ready.

"Three," Mikki called.

"Two," Zee said.

"One," Toni breathed.

Jayda jumped.

For a split second, there was nothing.

No ground. No sky. No sound but the rush of air filling her ears all at once.

Then everything arrived.

The rope caught clean and smooth, lifting her weight without warning. Her stomach flipped hard, the familiar drop of falling colliding with the unfamiliar steadiness of being held. Wind tore against her shirt and pressed her braids back from her face, beads clicking wildly like applause she hadn't earned yet.

She laughed, the sound ripped from her chest before she could decide if she meant to make it.

The yard streaked beneath her in blurred color. Green. Gold. Brown. The haystack rushed closer, then slowed, the line easing her down like it knew exactly when to let go.

For those seconds, Jayda was not performing.

She was not bracing.

She was not proving anything.

She was suspended between effort and release, between what she had always done and what she was just beginning to learn.

The rope hummed.

The trees stayed still.

The world held.

The world rushed around her.

Wind tore at her shirt. Her braids lifted behind her, weightless. Her stomach dropped, then soared. The trees blurred into streaks of green, the yard stretching and bending beneath her. For those few seconds, she was not loud or scared or brave on purpose.

She was flying.

The hay caught her with a thud and a cloud of dust. She landed flat on her back, eyes wide, chest heaving.

The girls ran toward her, laughing and shouting.

"You okay," Toni called.

Jayda blinked once.

Then she grinned.

"Again."

In that moment, the blueprint was no longer just lines on paper.

It was flight.

It was freedom.

It was proof that what they had built, with sweat and fear and hope, worked.

The word again did not echo the way Jayda expected it to.

It landed quietly, almost gently, like it was asking permission.

Mikki laughed first, relief breaking through her careful control. "One more," she said. "Then we reassess."

Jayda rolled onto her side and pushed herself up, hay clinging to her shirt and braids. Her legs felt strange, light and buzzy, like they did after running too hard and not stopping soon enough. She brushed straw from her arms and looked back up at the line.

It did not look different than it had before.

That was the part that surprised her.

Zee was already moving, checking the rope where it met the pulley, fingers sliding along the fibers with practiced attention. She tugged once, then again, listening more than watching. The rope answered with a steady resistance that eased something tight in her chest.

"Everything still feels good," Zee said.

Toni exhaled like she had been holding her breath for longer than she realized. She scribbled something in her notebook, then paused and crossed it out, rewriting it slower, neater.

Mikki checked the clipboard. The numbers had not changed. The angle still held. The distance still made sense. She told herself that meant something.

"All right," she said. "Same setup."

Jayda grinned and climbed back onto the platform without hesitation this time. Her movements were looser now, confidence humming just beneath her skin. She clipped in, tugged the harness once like she'd seen Zee do, then looked down again.

The ground did not feel as far away anymore.

"Whenever," she said.

They counted again.

This time, when Jayda jumped, she laughed the whole way down.

Not a scream. Not a shout.

A laugh that burst out of her chest like it had been waiting for this exact moment.

She landed cleaner this time, rolling onto her feet before dropping into the hay, breathless and bright.

"That's it," she said, pushing herself upright. "That's the one."

Mikki smiled, but she did not write anything down yet.

They ran the test twice more.

Once with Toni, who trusted the rope a little more each time, her hands shaking less, her laugh growing steadier. Once with Mikki, who stopped herself midline again, adjusting her grip and watching how the rope responded under controlled tension.

Each run ended the same way.

Solid. Predictable. Safe.

By the time the sun began to slide westward, the heat shifted, turning heavy again. Shadows stretched longer beneath the trees. The rope glowed faintly where the light caught it, bright against the bark.

They sat in the grass together, backs pressed to The Lookout, water bottles emptying fast.

"We should stop soon," Mikki said, though she did not sound eager to say it.

Jayda lay flat on her back, staring up through the leaves. "You always say that right when it gets good."

"That's how you keep it good," Zee said.

Jayda smiled, but she didn't argue.

Toni flipped to a new page in her notebook and drew the line again. Two trees. A rope. Four small figures beneath it. She added tiny arrows this time, showing motion instead of structure.

"This part," she said quietly, pointing. "This is where it changes."

Mikki leaned over to look. "Changes how."

Toni hesitated. "I don't know yet."

The silence that followed was not uncomfortable. It felt thoughtful. Like they were all listening for something just beneath the surface.

Jayda sat up and brushed hay from her legs. "One more," she said again, softer now.

Zee looked at Mikki.

Mikki looked at the rope.

She nodded. "Last one."

Jayda clipped in.

The air felt different this time. Not worse. Just alert.

They counted.

She jumped.

For a split second, everything was perfect.

Then the pulley groaned.

Not loud.

Just enough.

Zee's hands tightened instinctively on the rope, muscles bracing before her mind fully caught up. The line dipped a fraction lower than it had before, tension shifting through it like a ripple.

Jayda felt it too.

A brief drop. A change in speed. The smallest hitch before the line smoothed out again.

She landed safely, hay puffing up around her, heart pounding harder than it had the other times.

"You felt that," Mikki said.

Jayda nodded, sitting up slowly. "Yeah."

Zee was already at the rope, fingers moving fast, checking the pulley, the knot, the anchor point. Everything looked the same.

Too much the same.

"It held," Toni said.

"Yes," Zee said. "But it spoke."

They stood there for a moment, all of them staring at the line.

It was still.

Unbroken.

Working.

But no longer invisible.

Mikki exhaled slowly. "Okay," she said. "That's enough for today."

No one argued this time.

They unhooked the harness and lowered the rope carefully, movements slower now, more deliberate. Jayda helped coil it, hands quieter than usual. Toni packed her notebook away without writing another word.

As they finished, the yard returned to its ordinary shape. Trees. Grass. Rope no longer under tension.

But something had shifted.

Not failure.

Not fear.

Awareness.

As they headed toward the porch, Jayda glanced back once more at the line stretched between The Lookout and The Launch Tree.

It had carried her.

It had answered.

And now it waited.

The rope shifted slightly as a breeze moved through the yard.

Not enough to matter. Not enough to change anything. Just enough to remind them it wasn't fixed in place, that it responded to forces they couldn't see.

Toni noticed it first.

She paused mid sentence in her notebook, pencil hovering just above the page. The line swayed, barely perceptible, the pulley giving a soft metallic tick as it adjusted. She waited for Zee or Mikki to react.

They didn't.

Nothing was wrong.

Still, Toni wrote it down.

Jayda sat up straighter, following Toni's gaze. "It's fine," she said, though no one had asked. "Right."

Mikki nodded. "Wind does that."

Zee added, "Everything does something."

The breeze passed. The rope settled. The pulley went quiet again.

But the moment lingered.

Mikki stepped forward and ran her hand along the rope's length, not checking tension this time, just feeling. The fibers were warm, slightly rough, alive in a way numbers never captured. She stopped beneath The Launch Tree and looked up at the branch again, imagining weight there that wasn't yet.

"How many times do you think we can run it before we stop," Jayda asked.

Mikki considered the question longer than necessary. "Before or after something changes."

Jayda frowned. "What's supposed to change."

Mikki didn't answer right away. She glanced at Zee, then at Toni, then back at the rope.

"Nothing," she said finally. "That's the point."

Zee nodded. "You stop before it forces you to."

That landed.

Jayda lay back again, arms folded behind her head, staring up through the leaves. "So today," she said slowly, "we listen. Not just fly."

"Exactly," Zee said.

Toni closed her notebook for a moment, resting her palms on the cover like she was holding the thought in place. She didn't write this part down yet. Some things felt better kept intact until she knew where they belonged.

The yard went still again.

But now, the stillness had edges.

They all felt it.

And they all stayed anyway.

Mikki did not believe in luck.

She believed in numbers, in cause and effect, in systems that behaved the same way every time if you treated them correctly. But standing beneath the two trees, she felt something close to reverence anyway. The Lookout and The Launch Tree were not hers. They were older than her plans, older than the house, older than the idea of flight living inside her head. They had survived storms she could only imagine. Wind that bent branches without breaking them. Rain that soaked the ground so deeply roots had to choose where to cling.

That mattered.

She ran the numbers again, not because they were wrong, but because she needed to feel them settle. Forty feet. Angle adjusted by three degrees. Load limits written twice in the margin. The pencil paused in her hand as she stared up at the branch they had chosen, thick and solid, scarred but alive.

Trusting something bigger than yourself was different than trusting your own work.

Zee understood that instinctively.

She circled the base of The Lookout slowly, fingertips brushing the bark, eyes following the path of the branch overhead. She had learned long ago that structures told you things if you listened. Old wood spoke differently than new. Healthy fibers resisted in one way. Compromised ones gave in another. She pressed her palm flat against the trunk and closed her eyes for half a second, grounding herself before touching the rope again.

"This tree holds," she said quietly.

She was not guessing.

Jayda watched from a few steps back, arms crossed, head tipped upward. "Y'all act like it can hear you," she said, but there was no mockery in her voice. Only curiosity. "Like if you say the wrong thing, it'll drop us on purpose."

Toni smiled faintly. "Maybe it does," she said, scribbling something in the margin of her notebook. "Some people believe places remember how they're treated."

Jayda snorted. "Great. Now I gotta impress a tree."

But she shifted closer anyway.

Mikki adjusted the ladder angle by a fraction, aligning it with the trunk's lean instead of fighting it. "Systems work better when you don't force them," she said. "You work with what's already there."

She said it like it was about the build.

But all of them felt the weight of it land somewhere else too.

The pulley sat in Mikki's hands for a moment before she attached it, the metal warm from the sun. She turned it slowly, listening for resistance, for any hint of uneven movement. Satisfied, she clipped it into place and stepped back, eyes tracing the full line from anchor to launch, launch to landing.

The system existed now.

Not just pieces. Not just ideas.

A path.

The rope hummed faintly in the breeze, not moving, just alive enough to remind them it was there. Zee tightened the final anchor and tied the backup, fingers moving with calm precision. Toni documented the configuration carefully, labeling it System A, as if that meant there would be others later. Jayda stood between the trees, arms stretched wide, gauging distance with her body instead of a tape.

"Feels right," she said.

Mikki nodded slowly. "That's not math," she said.

Jayda grinned. "Still counts."

For the first time since they started, all four of them stood still together, looking at the same thing, seeing it not as parts but as a whole.

It wasn't ready yet.

But it was real.

Chapter 8
Practice Runs

The next morning felt easier than it should have.

The sun was already warm when they stepped back into Grandma Dot's yard, but the heat did not press the same way it had the day before. A light breeze moved through the trees, just enough to stir the leaves and lift the edge of Toni's notebook pages when she opened them. The rope hung between The Lookout and The Launch Tree exactly where they had left it, bright against the bark, quiet and waiting.

Nothing had shifted overnight.

That fact alone made Jayda grin.

"Well," she said, dropping her backpack near the porch steps, "if it broke while we were asleep, I would've liked a warning."

Mikki glanced up at the line automatically, eyes scanning the anchor points before she answered. "It didn't break," she said. "We lowered tension properly."

Jayda shrugged. "Still. Would've been rude."

Zee crouched near the base of The Lookout, running her fingers along the rope where it wrapped the trunk. She tugged once, then again, listening for resistance, for sound, for anything that felt different than it had yesterday.

"It's the same," she said.

That word mattered.

Same meant predictable. Same meant safe.

Same meant they could keep going.

They did not talk about flying right away.

Instead, they checked everything again.

Mikki set the ladder and climbed halfway up, stopping to inspect the pulley before going any higher. Toni knelt in the grass with her notebook open, sketching the setup as it stood now, not as it had yesterday. Zee retied one knot, not because it was wrong, but because she wanted to feel the rope move through her hands again. Jayda hovered nearby, handing things over when asked and pretending she was not counting how long this part took.

It was slower.

Deliberately so.

"That's the point," Mikki said when Jayda finally sighed. "Practice isn't supposed to feel exciting."

Jayda tilted her head. "That sounds fake."

Mikki smiled faintly. "It's still true."

Their first run of the morning was with weight.

Again.

A canvas bag, heavier this time, filled with books and a brick Jayda had found near the shed and insisted on adding "for realism." Zee clipped it in, stepped back, and nodded to Mikki.

"Ready."

Mikki raised her hand. "Three."

"Two," Zee said.

"One."

The bag slid smoothly across the line, the pulley humming instead of squeaking now. It landed in the hay with a dull, satisfying thump.

No flinch.

No freeze.

Jayda clapped anyway. "Ten out of ten. Would fly again."

"Not yet," Mikki said.

They ran it again.

And again.

By the third run, Toni's pencil moved faster, less hesitant. She wrote times without checking her numbers twice. Zee stopped retying between each test, trusting the knots she had already secured. Mikki stopped hovering over the clipboard and started watching the line instead.

The zipline did what it was supposed to do.

That was the strange part.

Nothing dramatic happened.

Nothing went wrong.

It worked.

The rope looked different when no one was touching it.

Without weight, without motion, it hung between The Lookout and The Launch Tree like a quiet line drawn across the afternoon. It did not hum now. It did not shift. It simply existed, sun catching on its fibers, bright against the bark.

Toni noticed that first.

She slowed as she packed her notebook away, eyes lingering on the line longer than necessary. Without the movement, without Jayda flying or Zee testing tension, *the rope felt less like a thrill and more like a sentence waiting to be finished.*

She did not write that down.

Mikki stood a few steps back, clipboard pressed to her chest, rereading numbers she already knew by heart. Everything still worked. The angles held. The load limits had not changed just because the day was ending.

That should have been comforting.

Instead, she felt the strange urge to check it one more time.

She didn't.

Learning when to stop was part of building too.

Zee coiled the extra rope with care, hands slower now, more deliberate. She had learned to trust her instincts, but she had also learned something else. Trust did not mean assuming nothing would ever go wrong.

It meant paying attention even when things went right.

Jayda lingered beneath the line, arms crossed loosely, head tipped back. The sky beyond the branches looked impossibly wide from that angle, blue stretching farther than she could follow.

"Tomorrow," she said, not asking a question.

Mikki nodded. "Tomorrow."

Zee glanced once more at the anchor point. "Tomorrow," she agreed.

Toni watched them, the word settling between the four of them like a quiet promise. Not reckless. Not rushed.

Earned.

As they turned toward the house, the rope stayed where it was, unmoving, patient.

It did not feel finished.

It felt like it was waiting.

By late morning, after several practice runs with weights, they were testing with people.

Carefully.

Zee went first, as always.

She clipped in, stepped off, slid halfway, then stopped herself easily, boots swinging just above the grass. She adjusted her grip and finished the run without a word.

"Still good," she said when she landed.

Toni went next.

She did not squeal this time. She slid farther than she had yesterday, landed clean, and laughed like she was surprised by herself.

Jayda whooped. "Look at you!"

Toni grinned, cheeks warm. "I didn't panic."

"That's growth," Jayda declared solemnly.

Mikki tested last.

She stopped midline again, just like before, watching the pulley respond under steady load. She listened, eyes narrowed, then released and landed.

She did not smile.

But she nodded.

They rotated like that for a while.

Zee. Toni. Mikki.

Jayda waited.

She always did.

By the time Mikki finally said, "Okay, Jayda," it felt less like permission and more like procedure.

Jayda clipped in without theatrics this time. She still grinned, still bounced on her toes once before stepping up, but the performance edge was gone. She had done this enough now to know what to expect.

That made it better.

They counted.

She jumped.

The ride felt smoother today. Faster, maybe, but more controlled. Jayda landed laughing, not because it was wild, but because it felt right.

Again.

They ran it again.

And again.

By the fourth run, Jayda stopped shouting on the way down. She focused instead, adjusting her body slightly, testing how small movements changed the ride. She landed and immediately turned back toward the platform.

"I think if I lean just a little," she said, already thinking out loud, "I can make it smoother at the end."

Mikki raised an eyebrow. "Or faster."

Jayda grinned. "Same thing."

Zee did not smile.

"Let's not experiment mid run," she said calmly. "Practice means repetition, not improvisation."

Jayda opened her mouth, then closed it again. "Okay. Fair."

They kept going.

Time slid forward without announcement.

The sun climbed, then drifted west. The breeze shifted. Shadows moved across the yard, stretching long beneath the rope. Toni filled three pages of notes and started a fourth. Mikki's clipboard grew heavier with numbers that no longer scared her. Zee's fingers moved with ease now, confident and sure.

The zipline became familiar.

That was the danger.

Not because it failed.

But because it didn't.

By early afternoon, they were no longer checking every detail between runs.

Not skipping.

Just trusting.

Mikki noticed it first.

She caught herself glancing at the clipboard instead of the rope during a test. She finished the run, then paused, pencil hovering.

"Hold on," she said.

Everyone stopped.

Jayda blinked. "What?"

Mikki frowned at the line. "We didn't recheck the anchor after the last three runs."

Zee stepped closer immediately, fingers already moving. She tugged, tested, listened.

"It's fine," she said.

Mikki nodded, but she did not relax right away. "I know. But we still should."

Jayda exhaled. "You're killing my momentum."

"That's my job," Mikki said.

They rechecked.

Nothing had changed.

Still, something settled in Mikki's chest that she could not quite name.

Not fear.

Awareness.

They took a break after that.

They ran it again.

Not because anyone said to, but because no one needed to say anything at all.

Jayda climbed back onto the platform with less ceremony this time. No speech. No dramatic pause. She clipped in, tugged the harness once, and nodded toward Mikki like they were confirming something already understood. When she stepped off, the line carried her exactly the way it had before. Same speed. Same arc. Same soft drop into the hay.

She landed, rolled once, and laughed, but the sound was different now. Lower. Shorter. Like the joy had settled somewhere deeper and didn't need to announce itself.

"That felt... normal," she said, brushing straw from her arms.

Mikki checked the clipboard anyway. The numbers matched. She hadn't really expected them not to. She marked the time, then stopped herself from checking it again. The urge passed quickly. The system was behaving. It had been for a while now.

Zee reset the line without being asked. Her hands moved from habit, not caution. The rope slid through her fingers smoothly, familiar in a way it hadn't been the first dozen times. She tested tension once instead of three times, then stepped back, eyes scanning the setup out of instinct more than concern.

"Good," she said, already turning away.

Toni watched all of it, pencil moving slower now. She still wrote everything down, but the urgency had softened. There were fewer arrows in the margins. Fewer circled notes. The sketch on the page looked cleaner, more confident, like it had decided what it wanted to be.

They ran it a third time.

Jayda didn't shout on the way down. Mikki didn't hold her breath. Zee didn't brace. The rope hummed once, steady and unremarkable, and the hay caught Jayda like it always did.

For the first time since they started building, no one rushed toward the line afterward.

They stood there instead, sweat dripping, hands sore, watching the system exist without asking anything from them.

It wasn't fragile anymore.

It was working.

Comfort can feel earned. They ran it again.

Not because anyone said to, but because no one needed to say anything at all.

Jayda climbed back onto the platform with less ceremony this time. No speech. No dramatic pause. She clipped in, tugged the harness once, and nodded toward Mikki like they were confirming something already understood. When she stepped off, the line carried her exactly the way it had before. Same speed. Same arc. Same soft drop into the hay.

She landed, rolled once, and laughed, but the sound was different now. Lower. Shorter. Like the joy had settled somewhere deeper and didn't need to announce itself.

"That felt... normal," she said, brushing straw from her arms.

Mikki checked the clipboard anyway. The numbers matched. She hadn't really expected them not to. She marked the time, then stopped herself from checking it again. The urge passed quickly. The system was behaving. It had been for a while now.

Zee reset the line without being asked. Her hands moved from habit, not caution. The rope slid through her fingers smoothly, familiar in a way it hadn't been the first dozen times. She tested tension once instead of three times, then stepped back, eyes scanning the setup out of instinct more than concern.

"Good," she said, already turning away.

Toni watched all of it, pencil moving slower now. She still wrote everything down, but the urgency had softened. There were fewer arrows in the margins. Fewer circled notes. The sketch on the page looked cleaner, more confident, like it had decided what it wanted to be.

They ran it a third time.

Jayda didn't shout on the way down. Mikki didn't hold her breath. Zee didn't brace. The rope hummed once, steady and unremarkable, and the hay caught Jayda like it always did.

For the first time since they started building, no one rushed toward the line afterward.

They stood there instead, sweat dripping, hands sore, watching the system exist without asking anything from them.

It wasn't fragile anymore.

It was working.

Not because anyone said they had to, but because their bodies asked for it all at once. They sat in the grass with their backs against The Lookout, passing around water bottles and a bag of chips Jayda had smuggled in her backpack.

"This feels official now," Toni said, flipping through her notes. "Like... we know what we're doing."

Jayda stretched out on the ground, hands folded behind her head. "I knew that yesterday."

Zee snorted softly. "You hoped that yesterday."

Jayda smiled. "Details."

Mikki stared up at the rope while she chewed, watching it sway slightly in the breeze. "It's supposed to feel boring at this stage," she said. "That means it's stable."

Jayda peeked at her. "You say boring like it's a compliment."

"It is."

They went back to work.

More runs.

More notes.

More confidence.

Jayda started timing herself without being asked. Toni sketched the motion of the pulley instead of just its placement. Zee adjusted her stance at the base of the ladder, moving instinctively into the best position to brace the line if needed.

Everything felt smooth.

Almost too smooth.

Late in the afternoon, when the light shifted again and the air cooled just enough to be noticeable, Jayda landed from another run and lay still in the hay for a second longer than usual.

"You okay," Toni asked.

Jayda nodded. "Yeah. Just thinking."

That alone made Mikki look up.

"About what," Zee asked.

Jayda sat up slowly, brushing hay from her arms. "About how this doesn't feel scary anymore."

No one answered right away.

"That's good," Toni said finally.

Jayda tilted her head. "Is it?"

Mikki closed her clipboard. "It can be."

Zee added, "It can also mean you stop listening."

Jayda considered that, then stood. "Okay. Then let's stop for today."

That surprised all of them.

Mikki blinked. "Really?"

Jayda shrugged. "We proved it works. We practiced. We're not rushing anything. That's the rule, right?"

Zee studied her face for a moment, then nodded. "That's the rule."

They packed up more slowly than usual.

The rope was lowered and coiled carefully. The harness hung on the porch railing. Toni tucked her notebook into her bag, pausing once to write a final line before closing it.

Practice makes patterns.

She underlined it twice.

As they headed inside, Jayda lingered for a moment, looking back at the space between the trees.

The zipline was no longer there.

But she could still feel it.

The way it had held her.

The way it had answered every time she trusted it.

That night, lying on the floor with her feet propped against the couch, Jayda stared at the ceiling and smiled.

Tomorrow, she thought, *we'll do it again.*

She did not hear the quiet warning beneath that thought.

Not yet.

Chapter 9
When Everyone Wants a Turn

The ice cream shop sat at the edge of town, tucked between a closed bait store and a laundromat that always smelled faintly of soap even from the parking lot. The windows were fogged from the cold inside, a sharp contrast to the heat pressing down on the sidewalk outside. A small bell jingled when they pushed the door open, and the sound felt brighter than it should have, like a celebration for something none of them had named out loud.

Jayda went first, leaning hard over the glass case like the decision mattered deeply. "Okay, but why do they expect you to choose when they got seventeen flavors and no samples," she said, squinting at the tubs.

"Because life is about commitment," Mikki replied, already counting cash in her hand.

Zee snorted quietly.

Toni hung back near the door, notebook tucked under her arm even though she knew she would not write right now. The air inside was cold enough to raise goosebumps along her arms, and she let herself feel it. The sharpness. The reset. Everything about today felt like that. Familiar, but just off enough to notice.

They ordered quickly after that. Chocolate for Mikki. Vanilla with rainbow sprinkles for Zee, predictable in the best way. Jayda changed her mind twice before landing on cookie dough, triumphant like she had won something. Toni chose strawberry, the color too bright to ignore.

They took their cones outside, stepping into the heat again. The cold sweetness melted fast, dripping down fingers and wrists. Jayda groaned dramatically as her scoop leaned sideways.

"This is disrespectful," she said, trying to save it. "I waited all day for this."

"You waited all day to fly," Mikki corrected.

Jayda grinned. "And this."

They found a narrow strip of shade along the side of the building and leaned against the warm brick, shoes scuffing the concrete. No one talked about the zipline right away. They talked about nothing. About how fast ice cream melted in summer. About how the shop still used paper napkins that stuck to your fingers. About how Zee somehow never dropped anything, no matter how slippery it got.

The laughter came easier than it had yesterday. Softer too. It did not explode out of them the way it had during the first flight. It settled instead, like something comfortable they were not afraid of losing.

Toni noticed that.

She noticed how Jayda did not pace while she talked. How Mikki leaned back instead of forward, shoulders loose. How Zee rested her weight on one leg, relaxed, eyes half lidded like she was listening without scanning for problems.

They looked like girls on summer break.

That felt new.

When they finished, Jayda crushed her napkin into a ball and tossed it into the trash with exaggerated focus. It bounced once, then dropped in.

"Perfect aim," she said.

"Don't start," Mikki warned.

They walked back toward Grandma Dot's house together, the road shimmering faintly with heat. Cicadas buzzed from the trees, loud and constant, a sound so familiar it barely registered until it stopped. The neighborhood felt slower at this time of day, like it had decided nothing urgent was allowed to happen before dinner.

They were halfway down the block when Malik appeared on the opposite sidewalk, hands shoved into his pockets, walking backward as he talked to the boys with him. There were three of them. Malik. Darius. Andre. All long-limbed and loud in that careless way that came from knowing they were being watched and liking it.

Malik spotted the girls first.

"Ohhh," he called out, drawing the word long and dramatic. "Look who it is."

Jayda groaned quietly. "Please keep walking."

Too late.

Malik turned fully around now, walking toward them with a grin that said he had been waiting for this moment. Darius snorted behind him, already laughing. Andre nudged Malik's shoulder like he was encouraging a performance.

"So," Malik said, slowing just enough to block the sidewalk. "Y'all building amusement parks now?"

Zee stopped short. "What are you talking about."

Malik tilted his head toward Grandma Dot's yard down the block. "Don't play innocent. I saw y'all back there the other day. Climbing trees. Rope everywhere. Looked like a whole situation."

Andre nodded. "Thought we was about to see somebody flying."

Jayda crossed her arms. "You were spying."

"I was observing," Malik said, putting on a mock serious voice. "There's a difference."

Mikki kept her face neutral. "And what exactly did you observe."

Malik grinned wider. "That y'all are absolutely not supposed to be doing whatever that was."

Darius laughed. "Facts."

There was a beat of silence. Then Jayda smiled, sharp and bright. "Good thing we didn't invite you."

Malik held a hand to his chest. "Wow. Hurtful."

Andre leaned closer to Darius. "Told you they dangerous."

Zee stepped around them. "We're going home."

Malik stepped aside, still smiling. "Yeah. I'd do the same. Before somebody gets famous for the wrong reason."

They kept walking. Malik's voice followed them down the block.

"Be careful, though," he called. "Gravity undefeated."

Jayda flipped him a lazy wave without turning around.

"Mind your business," she said.

Malik laughed, loud and easy, and the boys headed into the ice cream shop, the bell over the door jingling as it closed behind them.

The cicadas filled the space again.

Jayda walked ahead a little, swinging her arms, humming something tuneless under her breath. Zee stayed close to Mikki, their shoulders nearly brushing. Toni drifted behind them, watching the way the group naturally spaced itself without thinking.

She wondered when that had happened, when it had stopped being something they had to decide.

By the time the house came into view, the excitement from the shop had softened into something quieter. The porch steps waited in the shade. The yard stretched wide and green. The space between The Lookout and The Launch Tree was empty now, the rope gone, the air between them ordinary again.

Jayda slowed when she saw it.

"Huh," she said. "Looks smaller without it."

Mikki frowned slightly. "It's the same."

Jayda shrugged. "I know. Still."

They dropped their shoes by the porch and went inside for water, the cool of the house wrapping around them like a pause button. Glasses clinked. The sink ran. No one rushed.

When they stepped back out, the yard felt different than it had earlier. Not worse. Just quieter. Like it was holding its breath, waiting to see what they would do next.

Jayda flopped down on the grass without warning, arms spread wide. "I could nap right here."

Zee sat cross legged nearby. "You would wake up sunburned."

"Worth it."

Mikki stayed standing, eyes drifting automatically toward the trees before she caught herself. She leaned against the porch railing instead, folding her arms loosely.

Toni sat last, notebook still unopened in her lap.

No one said it, but all of them felt it.

The way the day was already tipping toward something else.

For a while, they stayed exactly where they were.

The grass was warm beneath them, flattened in places where the sun had pressed it down all afternoon. A breeze moved through the yard just enough to stir the leaves overhead, shadows shifting slowly across the ground. Somewhere down the block, a screen door slammed, followed by the distant sound of someone calling a name they all pretended not to hear.

Jayda rolled onto her side and propped herself up on one elbow. "So," she said, drawing the word out, "what do people do after they prove they can fly?"

Mikki glanced at her. "We didn't prove that."

Jayda grinned. "Speak for yourself."

Zee picked at a blade of grass, twisting it between her fingers. "You proved the system works," she said. "That's different."

Jayda considered that. "Still feels like something."

No one argued.

The yard felt bigger without the rope, the space between the trees open in a way that was almost uncomfortable. Toni found herself looking there again and again, expecting to see motion, to hear the faint hum of tension. Instead, there was only air. Ordinary and quiet.

She shifted her notebook on her lap but did not open it.

"You ever notice," Jayda said suddenly, "how the fun part is never the loudest part afterward?"

Mikki frowned. "What does that mean."

Jayda waved a hand vaguely. "Like... when you're on a roller coaster, and it stops, and everyone's screaming, but then there's that weird second when you're just sitting there and your legs feel wrong."

"That's adrenaline wearing off," Mikki said automatically.

Zee nodded. "Your body catches up before your brain does."

Jayda smiled. "See. That."

The quiet stretched again, not awkward, just present. Toni listened to the cicadas start up once more, their sound filling the space like static. It reminded her of how things settled after a storm, when everything looked the same but felt changed if you paid attention.

She wondered if the others felt it too.

Zee leaned back on her hands, eyes on the sky. "We did a lot in two days," she said.

Jayda scoffed lightly. "We built a zipline."

"And didn't break anything," Zee added.

"That's the real accomplishment," Mikki said.

Jayda laughed, then fell silent just as quickly. She plucked a piece of grass and flicked it away, watching where it landed. "It's weird," she said. "I thought I'd feel... I don't know. Bigger."

Mikki tilted her head. "Do you not?"

Jayda shrugged. "I feel the same. Just... steadier."

That made Toni look up.

Steadier felt like the right word.

Mikki leaned her head back against the porch post. "That's usually how it works," she said. "Big changes don't announce themselves."

Zee glanced at her. "You sound like your dad."

Mikki made a face. "I do not."

Jayda grinned. "You absolutely do."

They laughed again, the sound light and brief, like it didn't want to linger too long. When it faded, no one rushed to replace it.

Toni finally opened her notebook.

Not to write. Just to look at the last page she had filled earlier, the neat lines and arrows and labels already starting to feel like they belonged to yesterday. She traced one edge of the paper with her finger, then closed the book again.

"You gonna say something," Jayda asked, watching her.

Toni shook her head. "Not yet."

Zee nodded, like she understood exactly what that meant.

The sun dipped lower, light shifting gold through the leaves. Somewhere inside the house, a clock chimed once, marking the hour. It felt like a reminder, gentle but firm, that time was still moving even if they weren't.

Jayda stretched her arms over her head and sighed. "I don't want this part to end."

Mikki looked at her. "What part."

Jayda gestured around them. The yard. The house. The space they had made without realizing it. "This," she said simply.

No one answered right away.

But no one stood up either.

It was Jayda who said it first.

"Okay, but hear me out," she said, already sitting up straighter. "Ice cream."

Mikki blinked. "That's not a full sentence."

"It doesn't need to be," Jayda replied. "Ice cream after building a functional zipline feels earned."

Zee considered this seriously. "Cold would help," she said. "My hands are still buzzing."

Toni smiled a little. "Mine too."

That settled it faster than any vote ever could.

They cleaned up without talking much, moving through the motions like they had practiced them already. The harness was hung properly. The rope stayed coiled. The ladder leaned where it always did. Toni tucked her notebook into her bag, pressing it flat like she didn't want the pages to shift while she wasn't looking.

Grandma Dot waved them off from the porch, reminding them to be back before dinner and not to melt in the heat. Jayda promised they would do neither, which made Mikki snort.

The walk was short, but it felt different than usual.

The street buzzed with late afternoon noise. A lawn mower growled somewhere. A dog barked twice, then stopped. The pavement radiated heat up through their shoes, making the air shimmer just a little. Jayda walked ahead, swinging her arms wide, still restless even after hours of work.

"So," she said over her shoulder, "what flavor says 'successful engineering project.'"

Mikki sighed. "That's not how ice cream works."

Zee shrugged. "Chocolate. Always chocolate."

"Predictable," Jayda said affectionately.

Toni hesitated, then said, "Mint chip."

Jayda stopped short. "Really."

Toni nodded. "It feels... organized."

Mikki laughed before she could stop herself. "That actually makes sense."

The shop was cool inside, the kind of cool that made their skin prickle after the heat. The hum of the freezers filled the space, steady and comforting. They stood in line, reading flavors like they were choices that mattered more than they did.

Jayda changed her mind twice before ordering. Zee stuck with chocolate, no toppings. Mikki got vanilla and caramel, precise even in dessert. Toni ordered mint chip and watched the scoop land, clean and careful, like it belonged there.

They took their cones outside, perching on the low brick wall near the window. Ice cream dripped faster than expected, running down their fingers, sticky and cold.

Jayda licked her wrist and laughed. "Worth it."

For a while, they ate in silence, the kind that came from being full in more ways than one. Cars passed. Someone rode by on a bike, the chain rattling softly. The world kept moving, but it felt like it was doing so at a respectful distance.

Mikki was the first to notice.

She slowed, ice cream halfway to her mouth, eyes narrowing slightly. "Do you hear that."

Zee tilted her head. "Hear what."

Mikki listened again. "Nothing," she said finally.

Jayda frowned. "That's creepy."

"It's just quiet," Toni said. "Like... a pause."

Mikki nodded, but she didn't look convinced.

They finished their cones and tossed the napkins away, fingers still cold and sweet. The walk back felt slower, the sun lower now, shadows stretching longer across the sidewalk.

By the time Grandma Dot's house came back into view, the yard looked different.

Not changed.

Just waiting.

Jayda stopped at the gate and stared through it, a grin tugging at her mouth. "You know we're going to end up back there," she said.

Zee didn't argue.

Neither did Mikki.

Toni adjusted the strap of her bag and followed them in, the quiet from earlier trailing close behind.

They did not announce it.

No one said, Let's go check on it or Just one look. They simply drifted toward the yard like the decision had already been made somewhere beneath the talking.

The rope was still down.

Coiled neatly where Zee had left it.

The ladder rested against the fence instead of the tree, exactly as Mikki had insisted.

Everything looked smaller without the tension pulled tight between the trunks.

Jayda kicked off her sneakers and padded across the grass, the coolness making her sigh. "It's weird," she said. "Seeing it like this."

"Like what," Toni asked.

"Like a ride that's asleep," Jayda said, then laughed at herself. "Okay, that sounded creepy."

Zee crouched beside the rope again, fingertips brushing the coil. She didn't untie it. She didn't lift it. She just touched it, grounding herself the way she always did.

"It's resting," she said instead.

Mikki stood back near the porch, arms crossed loosely, eyes scanning the yard the way they always did now. Measurements lived in her head whether she invited them or not. Distances. Angles. What could change when you weren't watching.

Nothing changed, she told herself.

We put it away correctly.

That should have been enough.

Toni slipped her notebook out but didn't open it right away. She watched first. The way Jayda paced without pacing. The way Zee stayed low and still. The way Mikki kept her weight balanced, like she might need to move quickly.

They all looked different here than they had at the ice cream shop.

Quieter.

Sharper.

Jayda broke it first. "I'm not saying we should run it again," she said carefully, holding up a hand. "I'm just saying it feels... unfinished."

Zee glanced up. "It's finished for today."

Jayda nodded. "Yeah. I know. I just meant—" She waved a hand toward the trees. "Like, in my head."

Toni understood that immediately.

Some things didn't end just because you stopped touching them. Some things stayed active in your mind, replaying, adjusting, waiting for the next version of themselves.

She opened her notebook then and wrote one line, small and tucked into the corner of the page.

Some things don't stop just because you do.

She didn't underline it.

She didn't label it.

She let it sit.

Mikki stepped off the porch and joined them in the grass. "We did what we said we would," she said. "We practiced. We stopped when it was time."

Jayda looked at her. "And tomorrow."

Mikki hesitated just long enough for Zee to notice.

"Yes," Mikki said. "Tomorrow."

The word felt heavier now than it had earlier. Not dangerous. Just... loaded.

Zee stood and brushed grass from her hands. "If we come back out later," she said, "it's not to run it."

Jayda tilted her head. "Then what."

"To look," Zee said. "To notice."

Mikki considered that, then nodded. "Observation counts."

Jayda grinned. "Wow. We're officially the kind of people who say things like that."

They laughed softly, the sound easy and familiar, and for a moment the yard felt like it had before any of this had started. Just grass and trees and late summer light.

Still.

Waiting.

Toni closed her notebook and hugged it lightly to her chest. *This part matters too*, she thought. *The part where nothing happens.*

She didn't write that one down.

Not yet.

Chapter 10
Small Rules Get Bent

The morning did not feel urgent.

That was the first thing Mikki noticed.

Sunlight spilled across the kitchen floor in wide, lazy stripes, catching dust in the air and making it look like nothing had to be decided right away. Grandma Dot hummed softly at the stove, the sound steady and unbothered, like time itself had slowed down to match her pace.

Outside, the yard waited.

Jayda leaned against the counter, spinning a spoon between her fingers. "So," she said, casual like she hadn't been thinking about it all night, "are we officially good at this now."

Zee didn't look up from tying her shoelace. "We're practiced."

Jayda grinned. "Same thing."

"No," Mikki said automatically, reaching for her water bottle. "Not the same thing."

Jayda rolled her eyes, but there was no heat in it. "Okay, okay. Practiced. Still counts."

Toni sat at the table, notebook closed but present, her fingers resting lightly on the cover. She hadn't opened it yet. She didn't need to. *The day already felt written in a way she couldn't explain.*

The yard looked different when they stepped out.

Not because anything had changed.

Because they had.

The space between The Lookout and The Launch Tree no longer felt empty. Even without the rope pulled tight, the air carried memory. *Toni felt it immediately, like walking into a room where music had just stopped playing.*

Jayda saw it too.

She slowed, hands on her hips, eyes tracing the familiar path. "It's weird," she said. "I can still feel it."

Zee nodded once. "Muscle memory."

Mikki frowned slightly. "That's not—"

"Yes it is," Zee said calmly. "Your body remembers patterns faster than your brain trusts them."

Jayda snapped her fingers. "See. Science."

Mikki opened her mouth, then closed it again. She didn't argue. The numbers in her head lined up the way they always did, reassuring and quiet. Yesterday had ended clean. No failures. No surprises.

That mattered.

They moved automatically now.

The ladder shifted into place without discussion. The rope came out of its coil smoothly, familiar in Zee's hands. Toni set her notebook on the porch rail where she could reach it if she wanted to. Jayda stretched her arms overhead, rolling her shoulders like she was warming up for something that wasn't a performance anymore.

It felt easier.

That should have been comforting.

Instead, Mikki felt a faint pressure at the base of her neck, like a reminder she couldn't quite place.

She ignored it.

Not because it felt wrong.

Because nothing felt wrong at all.

The changes were small enough to feel accidental.

Jayda noticed it first, though she didn't say anything right away. The ladder leaned a little closer to the trunk than it had yesterday, angled just slightly inward. Not wrong. Just different. She shifted her weight from one foot to the other and watched Zee loop the rope over the branch.

"Did we always do it like that," she asked finally.

Zee glanced up, squinting once at the angle. "Close enough."

Mikki checked the clipboard out of habit, even though the page she needed wasn't there. She'd left it inside on purpose this time. "The angle's fine," she said. "It's actually more efficient."

Jayda grinned. "See. Upgrade."

Toni frowned, just a little. Not enough to interrupt. Enough to notice.

They ran the first test with weight like always. The canvas bag slid across the line smoothly, landing where it was supposed to with the same dull thump as yesterday.

No pause.

No freeze.

No flinch.

"That's what I'm talking about," Jayda said. "Consistency."

They ran it again.

This time, Mikki didn't write anything down.

She told herself she didn't need to. The numbers were the same. The timing felt right. She watched the rope instead of the margins, tracking the way it dipped and recovered, smooth and predictable.

Zee retied one knot instead of two.

She noticed herself doing it and almost laughed. The muscle memory had taken over. Her hands moved confidently, the rope sliding through her fingers without resistance.

"It's holding," she said, mostly to herself.

Toni opened her notebook and then closed it again.

She told herself she was just tired of documenting. That everything important had already been written down. Still, she shifted the notebook closer, resting her palm on the cover *like she might need it quickly.*

Jayda climbed the ladder before anyone told her to stop.

Not all the way. Just a few rungs. Just enough to test the feel of it beneath her feet.

"Hey," Mikki said. "We said order."

Jayda froze, then laughed. "Relax. I'm not jumping. I just wanted to—"

"Feel it," Zee finished.

Jayda nodded. "Exactly."

Zee didn't tell her to get down.

That was new.

Jayda climbed back down and dusted off her hands like it proved something. "Feels solid."

Mikki didn't argue. She checked the rope once more, tugged lightly, then nodded.

"Okay," she said. "Human test."

They rotated.

Zee went first. Clean. Controlled. No adjustments needed.

Toni followed. A little faster than yesterday. She laughed when she landed, surprised by how easy it felt.

Mikki tested last, stopping herself midline like always. She listened, counted in her head, then released.

Everything behaved.

Jayda waited, bouncing once on her heels, then stilling herself. "Can I go."

Mikki hesitated.

Not long enough to matter.

Just long enough to notice.

"Yes," she said.

Jayda clipped in and jumped without ceremony.

The ride was smooth. Familiar. Almost boring.

She landed and didn't shout.

"That's wild," she said. "I barely felt it."

Zee nodded. "That's what happens when a system settles."

Toni swallowed.

Settled sounded permanent.

They ran it again.

And again.

Between runs, no one reset the anchor.

No one said they should.

The rope didn't complain.

That was the problem.

They stopped counting after the fifth run.

Not on purpose. It just happened quietly, the way habits do when no one is watching them form.

Jayda climbed, clipped in, jumped. Landed. Smiled. Walked back around without waiting for anyone to say her name. Zee reset the rope with a single practiced motion instead of the careful two-step she had used before. Mikki glanced at the line, then at Jayda, then nodded like the order was already decided.

Toni noticed first that no one said ready anymore.

The word had slipped out of use, unnecessary now that everything felt predictable. The rope behaved the same way each time. The pulley hummed softly, steady and unremarkable. The hay caught Jayda clean, just like it had every other time.

Predictable felt earned.

Predictable felt safe.

Predictable felt permanent.

Jayda ran it again.

This time she leaned forward just a little, adjusting her weight the way she'd mentioned before. Nothing dramatic happened. The ride ended exactly where it always did.

"See," she said, brushing hay from her arms. "Told you."

Mikki watched the rope instead of Jayda's face. "Don't change things mid-run," she said, but her voice lacked the sharp edge it would have had yesterday.

Jayda grinned. "I barely did."

Zee tightened the line once, more out of habit than concern. She didn't test it again. Her hands already knew what to expect.

It's holding, she thought. *It's been holding.*

Toni shifted where she sat on the porch steps, notebook balanced on her knee. She had written less this morning than she had planned. The page was half empty, the lines spaced wider than usual.

Nothing new to say, she told herself.

Still, her eyes kept drifting to the anchor point. The knot looked the same. The rope lay the same way against the bark. But the stillness around it felt louder now, like silence right before someone speaks.

Jayda climbed again.

"Last one," Mikki said automatically.

Jayda laughed. "You said that two runs ago."

Mikki paused, then smiled. "Okay. One more after this."

Zee glanced at her, then away.

Jayda jumped.

The rope dipped.

Not enough to alarm anyone. Just enough to register.

Jayda landed safely, laughing, rolling once before popping back up to her feet. "Okay, now that one felt different."

Mikki frowned. "Different how."

Jayda shrugged. "Faster, maybe."

Zee crouched and checked the rope where it wrapped the trunk, fingers sliding along the fibers. Everything felt the same. No fray. No shift. No sound.

"It's fine," she said.

Mikki nodded, though she hadn't realized she was holding her breath until she let it out. "Yeah. Fine."

Toni pressed her pencil harder into the page and drew a small circle around the anchor point. She didn't label it. She didn't know why she'd marked it at all.

If nothing's wrong, she thought, *why does it feel like something just moved.*

Jayda was already climbing again.

No one stopped her.

No one said wait.

The system didn't complain.

That was the part that mattered.

They all felt it now.

Not as fear. Not yet. More like a low vibration under everything else, the way a train announces itself before you ever see it. The zipline stood between The Lookout and The Launch Tree, quiet and cooperative, the rope stretched clean and bright against the bark.

Jayda broke the silence first, because she always did.

"So," she said, rocking back on her heels, "are we done done, or just done for now."

Mikki glanced at the rope, then at the space beneath it. "We've run it enough times," she said. "The system's stable."

Zee didn't answer right away. She knelt near the base of the tree, fingers brushing the rope where it wrapped around the trunk. The fibers were warm from the sun and from use. Familiar. Too familiar.

Stable isn't the same as finished, she thought.

Toni watched her, the notebook pressed lightly to her stomach. She hadn't meant to hold it that way. It just felt safer there.

Jayda grinned. "So that's a yes."

Mikki hesitated.

Just a fraction of a second.

Enough for Toni to notice.

"We could do one more," Mikki said finally. "Just to be sure."

Zee looked up sharply. "One more what."

"One more run," Mikki said. "Same setup. Same conditions."

Jayda's smile widened. "I volunteer."

Of course she did.

Zee stood slowly, brushing dirt from her knees. "If we do another," she said, choosing her words carefully, "we reset everything first."

Jayda groaned. "Again?"

"Yes," Zee said. "Again."

Mikki nodded. "That's fair."

They reset.

Not as thoroughly as they had the first time that morning. Not because they were careless. Because everything already looked right. The ladder stayed where it was. The pulley stayed clipped. Zee retied the anchor once instead of twice. Mikki checked the angle with her eyes instead of measuring.

Toni noticed every shortcut.

She didn't say anything.

I don't know enough yet, she told herself. I just notice things.

Jayda clipped in, movements quick and confident. She tugged the harness once, not twice. Looked back at the others.

"You ready."

Mikki raised her hand. "Three."

"Two," Zee said.

"One."

Jayda jumped.

For the first second, everything felt the same.

The rope caught clean. The pulley rolled smooth. Jayda's body moved into the familiar arc, breath whooshing out of her chest as the ground slid away beneath her.

Then the line shuddered.

Just once.

A small, sharp vibration that traveled through the rope and into Zee's hands before anyone else could react.

Zee's grip tightened instinctively, muscles bracing. The rope dipped lower than it had before. Not dangerously. Not dramatically.

But different.

Jayda felt it.

Her stomach dropped harder than usual, the rhythm of the ride shifting just enough to steal the laugh from her throat. She grabbed the rope with both hands, heart hammering.

Then it smoothed out.

The system corrected itself.

Jayda landed safely in the hay, rolling onto her side and sitting up slowly. Dust puffed into the air around her.

For a moment, no one spoke.

"You good," Toni asked, voice too quick to hide.

Jayda nodded, but she didn't grin. "Yeah. I'm good."

Mikki stepped forward. "The load held."

Zee didn't move from her spot. Her eyes stayed on the rope. On the way it rested now, perfectly still again, like nothing had happened.

It answered, she thought. *But it spoke louder this time.*

Toni's chest felt tight.

That wasn't nothing, she thought. *That was a warning.*

Jayda stood and brushed hay from her arms. "It felt... off," she admitted. "Just for a second."

Mikki frowned. "It recovered immediately."

"I know," Jayda said. "I'm just saying I noticed it."

Zee finally looked at them. "That's enough for today."

Jayda didn't argue.

Neither did Mikki.

They stood there together, the zipline quiet between them, the late afternoon sun catching on the rope like it always had.

Working.

Holding.

But no longer silent.

And all of them understood, without saying it out loud, that something had shifted.

Chapter 11
Almost

The house felt different once the door closed behind them.

Not quieter exactly. Just slower. Like the walls had decided to hold onto the day instead of letting it spill back out. Shoes were kicked off near the door in uneven pairs. Someone dropped a backpack with a soft thud. The ceiling fan turned lazily overhead, stirring air that still smelled faintly like sun and grass.

Mikki noticed it first.

Her body was tired, but her mind had not followed suit. Numbers still lined up behind her eyes. Angles. Timing. The way the rope had behaved the last three runs. She told herself she was done thinking about it, that they had stopped at the right moment.

Stopping counts too, she reminded herself.

Jayda flopped onto the rug like gravity had finally remembered her. She stared at the ceiling, arms spread wide, chest rising and falling fast enough to be noticeable.

"That was a lot," she said.

Zee sat cross legged nearby, back straight, hands resting loosely on her knees. She nodded once. "It was."

Toni hovered near the couch, notebook still in her bag. She had not touched it since they came inside. The urge was there, buzzing under her skin, but she resisted it. Writing would turn the day into something finished.

She wasn't ready for that yet.

For a few minutes, no one spoke.

The clock on the wall ticked.

Not evenly. Not gently.

Tick. Ticktick. Tick.

Each second landed wrong, sharp and misplaced, like it was trying to remind them that the world was still moving even though they were not. The sound filled the room, bouncing faintly off the walls, slipping into the spaces where no one was talking.

A car passed outside, tires hissing over the road. The engine rose, then faded, the noise stretching out longer than it should have, like it was reluctant to leave. For a moment, its presence pressed against the house, and then it was gone, leaving behind the hollow quiet that always followed something leaving too quickly.

Somewhere deeper in the house, Grandma Dot moved around the kitchen. A cabinet opened. Closed. The soft clink of dishes followed, ceramic touching ceramic, careful and unhurried. The sound carried down the hallway in small, ordinary pieces, steady enough to feel intentional.

Life, continuing.

The clock kept ticking.

The car was already blocks away.

The dishes clinked again, a plate set down, a spoon nudged aside.

Nothing had stopped.

Only them.

Jayda broke the silence first. "I don't feel how I thought I would."

Mikki glanced at her. "How did you think you'd feel."

Jayda shrugged without looking away from the ceiling. "I don't know. Bigger. Like something would be different."

Zee tilted her head. "Something is different."

Jayda frowned. "Yeah, but I can't point to it."

That landed heavier than any of them expected.

Toni sat down slowly, folding her legs beneath her. *Different without a name was the hardest kind,* she thought. You couldn't argue with it. You couldn't solve it.

Mikki leaned back against the couch, eyes closed for a second longer than usual. *Everything worked,* she told herself again. *That matters.*

It should have been enough.

But the feeling didn't leave.

It stayed, quiet and patient, settling into the room the same way the dust had settled in the sunlight that morning.

Not asking for attention.

Just waiting.

Grandma Dot did not ask questions.

That alone felt like a decision.

She set a pitcher of water on the table and left it there, condensation already sliding down the sides, then moved back to the stove like nothing unusual had happened. The smell of something warm and familiar drifted through the house, grounding in a way none of them commented on.

Jayda sat up and grabbed a glass, draining half of it in one go. "I'm starving," she said. "Like... more than normal."

Zee poured herself a smaller glass and sipped slowly. "Adrenaline crash," she said. "Your body's catching up."

Jayda made a face. "I don't like when my body does things without checking first."

Mikki almost smiled.

Instead, she watched the way the water sloshed slightly when Jayda set the glass down. She watched the line it left on the table, the faint ring forming beneath it. *Everything leaves a mark,* she thought, and immediately didn't like where that idea was going.

Toni stood and crossed the room, pulling her notebook out at last. She didn't open it. She just held it, fingers curled around the edge like an anchor.

"I keep thinking about the space," she said.

Zee looked up. "What space."

"Between the trees," Toni said. "When the rope's not there."

Jayda blinked. "That's... weirdly specific."

Toni nodded. "I know."

The room went quiet again, but this time it felt sharper. Like someone had named the thing they were all circling without meaning to.

Mikki cleared her throat. "Empty space always feels bigger once you've filled it," she said. "Your brain remembers what used to be there."

Zee considered that. "Or it remembers what could be there again."

Jayda laughed softly, but it didn't last. "Okay, but that's creepy."

Or honest, Toni thought.

She finally opened the notebook, flipping past pages she already knew by heart. Diagrams. Notes. Small observations that had felt urgent at the time. She stopped on a blank page.

The pen hovered.

She didn't write.

Outside, the light shifted again, sliding lower, softer. Shadows stretched across the yard, touching the place where the rope had hung like they were checking something for themselves.

Mikki stood and moved to the window without realizing she was doing it. She rested her hand against the glass, watching the trees sway slightly in the breeze.

We did everything right, she told herself.

The thought didn't feel as solid as it had earlier.

Zee noticed her first. "You okay."

Mikki nodded. "Yeah. Just tired."

It was true.

It just wasn't the whole truth.

The day wasn't finished with them yet.

It had simply followed them inside.

As dusk settled, they went back into the yard without deciding to.

It happened the way habits do, quietly and without ceremony. Jayda stepped off the porch first, bare feet pressing into the grass like she was checking the temperature of something. Zee followed, hands in her pockets, eyes already moving over the trees. Mikki came last, pausing at the edge of the porch as if she were crossing an invisible line. Toni brought up the rear, notebook tucked under her arm, unopened but present.

The yard looked harmless.

That was the problem.

The rope was still coiled where Zee had left it, pale against the darker grass. The ladder rested against the fence instead of the tree, exactly where Mikki had insisted it should go. Everything was orderly. Everything was calm.

Jayda nudged the rope with her toe. "We're not running it," she said quickly. "I just wanted to... see it."

"Seeing turns into touching," Mikki said.

Zee nodded. "And touching turns into testing."

Jayda held up both hands. "Observation only. I swear."

No one stopped her when she crouched down.

That should have been the warning.

Zee moved closer, kneeling beside her. She didn't pick the rope up, but her fingers hovered just above it, muscle memory twitching like it wanted permission. "The fibers feel warmer than earlier," she said. "From use."

"That's normal," Mikki replied immediately.

Zee looked at her. "I didn't say it wasn't."

Jayda glanced between them. "Okay, why does this feel like when adults say they're 'just talking.'"

Toni shifted her weight. Her notebook pressed against her ribs, suddenly heavier. She pulled it out without thinking and flipped to the blank page she had opened earlier. She didn't write yet. She waited.

Mikki stepped closer to the anchor point, eyes narrowing. The knot looked the same. The bark beneath it bore the same shallow grooves. But the ground beneath the tree felt softer under her shoes than it had that morning.

"Did anyone notice the dirt here earlier," she asked.

Zee pressed her palm into the ground once, then again. "It's looser," she said. "Probably from yesterday's runs."

"Probably," Jayda echoed.

The word didn't settle.

Toni finally wrote, small and careful.

Almost isn't nothing.

She closed the notebook again.

It happened fast.

Jayda reached for the rope without thinking, fingers closing around it like they had done a hundred times already. She didn't pull. She didn't lift. She just tested the weight of it in her hands.

The rope shifted.

Not dramatically. Not dangerously.

Just enough.

The coil loosened and slid a few inches across the grass, the sound soft but unmistakable. Zee's head snapped up. Mikki inhaled sharply. Jayda froze, fingers still wrapped around the fibers.

"I didn't—" Jayda started.

"I know," Zee said, already moving.

The rope bumped lightly against the ladder where it leaned against the fence. The ladder rocked once.

Once was enough.

Mikki lunged forward and grabbed it before it could tip, heart slamming so hard it hurt. The ladder settled back into place, obedient and still.

Silence dropped hard and sudden.

Jayda let go of the rope like it had burned her. "I didn't mean to," she said, voice too quick. "I wasn't even pulling."

"That's the point," Zee said, standing now. Her voice was calm, but her jaw was tight. "You didn't mean to."

Toni felt the moment stretch, thin and sharp. This was it. This was the place where things split.

Mikki straightened slowly, hands still braced on the ladder. "That could have tipped," she said. "If I hadn't been right here—"

"But it didn't," Jayda said, a little too defensively. "Nothing happened."

Zee turned on her. "Something almost happened."

Jayda crossed her arms. "You're acting like it was about to collapse."

"I'm acting like systems don't care about intentions," Zee snapped. Then she stopped, breathing hard. "I'm sorry. I just—"

"You're scared," Jayda said.

Zee didn't deny it.

Toni stepped forward before she could talk herself out of it. "That's what an almost is," she said quietly. "It's the thing that tells you what could happen next."

Mikki nodded slowly. "We don't get credit for stopping something we didn't see coming. We only get credit for noticing."

Jayda looked down at the grass. "I wasn't trying to be reckless."

"I know," Zee said. "But confidence can look like carelessness when it goes unchecked."

That hurt.

They all felt it.

Toni opened her notebook again, hands shaking just slightly, and wrote:

Almost is where stories change.

She underlined it once.

They moved away from the setup together.

Not dramatically. Not in anger.

Just... deliberately.

Mikki carried the ladder back to the shed herself, setting it down with more care than necessary. Zee recoiled the rope tighter this time, looping it slower, testing the tension even though it wasn't under load. Jayda stood off to the side, arms wrapped around herself, watching every movement like she was trying to learn something without touching it again.

Toni didn't help. She observed.

That felt important.

When everything was put away again, the yard looked empty in a different way than before. Not waiting. Not inviting.

Closed.

Jayda broke the silence first. "I don't like that I didn't feel nervous," she said. "Not even a little."

"That doesn't mean you were wrong," Mikki said carefully. "It means your warning system adjusted."

"And maybe adjusted too far," Zee added.

Jayda swallowed. "I thought that meant I was getting better."

"You are," Toni said. "But getting better doesn't mean skipping the part where you're careful."

Jayda looked at her. "You always know when to say stuff like that."

Toni shrugged. "I write it down until it makes sense."

Zee exhaled slowly. "We stop here," she said. "Not because something broke. Because it didn't."

Mikki nodded. "That's the rule now."

Jayda kicked at the grass once, then stilled herself. "Okay," she said. "I get it."

The word landed heavier than agreement.

It meant responsibility.

Toni closed her notebook and hugged it lightly to her chest. She didn't write the last thought that formed, but it stayed with her anyway.

Almost is the sound of the future knocking.

The yard stayed quiet.

Not because nothing could happen.
But because they had learned how close it already had come.

Chapter 12
The Day the Wind Changed

The morning arrived the way mornings always did at Grandma Dot's house, quiet and unannounced.

Sunlight filtered through the kitchen window, pale and steady, warming the edge of the table and the backs of the chairs. The radio played softly from the counter, a voice talking about nothing urgent. Grandma Dot moved between the sink and the stove with the same unhurried rhythm as always, her slippers whispering against the floor.

Nothing felt different.

That was what made Mikki uneasy.

She stood at the back door, hand resting on the frame, looking out into the yard. The grass lay flat where they had walked it down the day before. The trees stood where they always had. The space between The Lookout and The Launch Tree looked ordinary again, empty and harmless.

Everything's the same, she told herself.

Jayda burst through the screen door behind her, already halfway outside. "If it's already hot, I'm not wearing socks," she announced, kicking her shoes off onto the porch.

Zee followed more quietly, pausing at the threshold like she always did, eyes scanning the yard without looking like she was scanning. Toni came last, notebook tucked under her arm, fingers curled around the edge like it was something she might drop if she wasn't careful.

The breeze brushed past them as they stepped out.

It wasn't strong. It wasn't sudden. Just enough to move the leaves overhead and lift the loose ends of Toni's hair against her cheek. The sound it made was soft, familiar, easy to ignore.

Jayda tilted her face toward it. "At least it's not dead air today."

Zee didn't answer. She was watching the rope.

They hadn't pulled it tight yet. It still hung slack between the trees, looped but resting, pale against the bark. As the breeze passed through the yard, the rope shifted slightly, swaying just enough to catch the light.

It made a sound.

Not loud. Not sharp. Just a low, brief hum, like a string brushed by accident.

Mikki stiffened.

"Did you hear that," she asked.

Jayda shrugged. "Hear what."

"The rope," Mikki said.

Zee nodded once. "It moved."

"That's normal," Jayda said easily. "It's outside."

Mikki knew that. She did. Wind moved things. That was basic. Predictable.

Still, she watched the rope longer than she meant to.

The breeze came again, a little steadier this time. Leaves whispered overhead. Shadows shifted across the grass, sliding farther than they had a moment ago. The rope lifted and settled again, tapping lightly against the trunk before going still.

No one had touched it.

Toni felt it then, the small click in her chest that came when something didn't line up the way it should. Not wrong enough to name. Just different enough to notice.

It sounds different when it's not waiting for us, she thought.

She didn't write it down.

Jayda dropped onto the porch steps and stretched her legs out in front of her. "Okay, so," she said, rocking back on her hands, "are we actually doing anything yet, or are we just staring at it like it's going to blink first."

Zee crouched near the base of The Lookout, resting her palm lightly against the bark. The tree felt solid. Unmoved. The kind of steady you trusted without thinking.

"The wind's picking up," she said.

Mikki glanced up at the sky. It was clear. Blue. Nothing chasing anything else across it.

"It's not supposed to," she said.

Jayda snorted. "Wind doesn't RSVP."

Another gust moved through the yard, stronger this time. The rope lifted higher, twisting slightly before settling back into place. The pulley gave a faint click where it rested, metal adjusting to motion it hadn't been carrying a minute ago.

The yard went quiet again.

Not silent. Just waiting.

Toni shifted her weight, eyes moving between the trees, the rope, the shadows that no longer sat where they had a moment earlier.

This isn't dramatic, she told herself.
This is just different.

Mikki stepped off the porch, closer to the setup than she'd planned. She didn't touch anything. She just stood there, watching the way the breeze moved through the space like it belonged to someone else.

"Let's just keep an eye on it," she said finally.

Zee nodded. "Yeah."

Jayda leaned back on her elbows. "See. Fine."

The wind passed through again, light but insistent, and this time it didn't feel like background anymore.

It felt like the day had decided to join them.

And none of them could quite explain why that mattered yet.

They treated the wind like a variable.

That was the mistake.

Mikki said it first, kneeling near the base of the ladder with her eyes narrowed at the angle. "It's not strong," she said. "It's inconsistent. That's easier to work with."

Jayda perked up immediately. "See. Manageable."

Zee didn't answer right away. She watched the leaves instead, the way they shifted in uneven waves. Some branches barely moved. Others bent and swayed like they were listening to something different.

"Inconsistent means unpredictable," Zee said finally.

Mikki shook her head. "Only if you don't account for it."

She adjusted the ladder slightly, moving it a few inches farther from the trunk. The shift was small, careful, the kind that made sense on paper. Zee followed her lead, lifting the rope and resetting the loop so it sat cleaner against the bark.

Nothing resisted.

That felt reassuring.

Jayda stood back, hands on her hips, watching them work. "So we're not stopping," she said. "We're just... tuning."

"Tuning," Mikki echoed, nodding. "Exactly."

Toni hovered near the porch, notebook still closed. She watched the rope respond to each adjustment, the way it lifted and settled with the breeze. It looked cooperative. Easy.

Too easy.

It's not waiting for us today, she thought. It's responding to everything.

The wind came again, stronger this time, pushing through the yard with more confidence. The rope swayed, then stilled. The pulley clicked softly, adjusting without complaint.

Zee tightened the anchor once more, pulling the rope through her hands until the tension felt familiar again. She tested it twice. Then stopped herself from testing a third time.

"It's good," she said.

Jayda smiled. "See. The system knows what it's doing."

Mikki straightened, brushing dirt from her knees. "Systems don't know," she said. "They behave."

Jayda waved that off. "Same thing."

Zee didn't correct her.

They ran the first test with weight.

The canvas bag slid across the line smoothly, just as it had before. The wind nudged it midline, shifting its path by inches instead of feet. It landed clean, the pulley humming a little longer than usual before settling.

No one flinched.

"That was fine," Jayda said quickly.

Mikki nodded. "Within tolerance."

Zee crouched near the anchor again, fingers brushing the rope. It felt warm now. Not hot. Just... alive in a way it hadn't been yesterday.

"It moved more," Toni said quietly.

Jayda looked at her. "Because of the wind."

"Yes," Toni said. "I know."

They ran the test again.

This time, Mikki adjusted her stance without realizing it, widening her feet like she was bracing for something heavier. The bag dipped lower at the center of the line before correcting itself, swinging slightly before settling.

Still fine.

Still working.

Jayda clapped once. "Okay, but that was cool."

Zee didn't smile.

She watched the rope after the bag landed, the way it continued to sway even after the weight was gone. The movement lingered longer than it should have, like the system was slower to forget.

"The wind's not steady," she said. "It's shifting direction."

Mikki checked the sky again. "That happens."

"Yes," Zee said. "But it means the load isn't consistent."

Jayda crossed her arms. "So what, we just don't do anything if the weather isn't perfect."

"No," Mikki said. "We adjust."

Toni felt the tension settle between them, thin but present. Adjusting sounded responsible. Smart. Like progress.

But it also meant something else.

Adjusting means we think we're in control, she thought.

She pressed her fingers into the notebook cover, grounding herself.

They reset the rope again. Not from scratch. Just enough to feel like they were responding instead of ignoring.

That mattered to all of them.

When the rope was tight again, the wind passed through once more, tugging at it like a quiet test. The system responded smoothly, flexing and settling like it had learned how to move with it.

Jayda grinned. "Look at that. It's cooperating."

Zee glanced at Mikki.

Mikki hesitated, just a fraction of a second, then nodded. "Okay," she said. "One more test."

No one asked what kind.

They all knew.

The wind didn't stop.

It didn't grow dramatic either.

It just stayed.

And somewhere between the adjusting and the nodding and the quiet confidence settling back into place, the line between caution and comfort thinned again.

Not enough to break.

Just enough to bend.

They didn't say *human test*.

No one needed to.

Jayda stepped forward like the decision had already been made somewhere behind her ribs. Not eager. Not reckless. Just ready in the way people get when they've done something enough times that it feels like muscle memory instead of choice.

"I can go," she said.

Mikki didn't answer right away. She watched the rope instead. The wind tugged at it again, light but insistent, like it was asking a question instead of making a demand.

"Same setup," Mikki said finally. "No changes mid-run."

Jayda nodded. "Same."

Zee clipped the harness with deliberate care, fingers moving slower than before. She tested the connection once. Then again.

She stopped herself before a third.

It's fine, she told herself. It's been fine.

Toni stayed near the porch, notebook pressed against her stomach. She didn't open it. She didn't trust her hands to stay steady enough yet.

Jayda climbed the ladder without hurry. She paused at the top, not for drama, but to feel the wind against her face. It pushed past her shoulder, tugged lightly at her shirt, then slipped away again.

"That's new," she said.

Mikki looked up. "What."

"The wind," Jayda said. "You can feel it up here more."

"That makes sense," Mikki replied. "Elevation."

Zee didn't like that answer.

"Ready," Jayda said anyway.

They didn't count out loud this time.

Jayda stepped off.

The rope caught clean.

The pulley rolled smooth.

For the first few seconds, everything felt exactly the same. Familiar arc. Familiar speed. Jayda's body settled into the movement like it always did, breath whooshing out as the ground slid away beneath her.

Then the wind shifted.

Not sharply.

Not violently.

Just enough to push sideways instead of straight through.

The rope swayed.

Barely.

Jayda felt it first, a subtle change in rhythm that didn't register as fear so much as surprise. Her grip tightened automatically. Her body adjusted without thinking, shoulders angling just slightly to compensate.

Okay, she thought. *I've got this.*

Below, Zee's stance widened. She hadn't planned to move, but her body did it anyway, responding to the way the rope pulled differently against the anchor.

Mikki's eyes tracked the line, pulse ticking faster than she liked. The dip at the center was lower than the last run. Not dangerous.

But noticeable.

Toni's breath caught.

It's still holding, she told herself. It's still holding.

The pulley hummed louder this time, the sound stretching out longer than it should have. The wind pushed again, nudging Jayda just enough that her landing path shifted a foot to the left.

Jayda landed safely.

She stumbled once, then caught herself, boots skidding slightly in the grass before she steadied.

No fall.

No collapse.

Just... movement.

They all froze.

Jayda straightened slowly, heart thudding harder now. "That was different," she said.

Mikki exhaled. "But controlled."

Zee didn't respond immediately. She watched the rope continue to sway after Jayda had stepped away, the motion lingering like a thought that hadn't finished forming.

"It corrected," Mikki added, more firmly this time.

Jayda nodded, trying to smile. "Yeah. It corrected."

Toni finally spoke. "It didn't feel the same."

Jayda looked at her. "No," she admitted. "It didn't."

The wind moved through the yard again, lifting leaves, shifting shadows. The rope answered, flexing gently, settling back into place like it always did.

Still working.

Still cooperating.

Mikki stepped closer to the anchor, checking the knot with her eyes instead of her hands. Everything looked right. Everything *was* right.

"That's what systems do," she said, more to herself than anyone else. "They adjust."

Zee's jaw tightened. "Until they don't."

Jayda rubbed her palms against her shorts, grounding herself. "So what, we stop every time it feels a little off."

"No," Mikki said. "We note it."

Toni felt something twist in her chest.

Noting isn't the same as stopping, she thought.

But she didn't say it.

The wind eased, just slightly, like it was satisfied for now.

Jayda looked back at the ladder. Then at the rope. Then at her friends.

"It still works," she said.

That was the truth.

And it was the most dangerous part.

Because everything that mattered most was still standing.

No one said stop.

That was how it happened.

They stood there, the rope swaying gently between The Lookout and The Launch Tree, the wind easing and returning in uneven breaths. The system had adjusted. It had answered. Everyone could see that.

Jayda broke the silence first, because silence had never been her strength. "Okay," she said, rubbing her hands together, "so that was different, but not bad different."

Zee looked at her sharply. "Different is different."

"But it still worked," Jayda said. "I landed. The rope held. The anchor didn't budge."

Mikki nodded slowly. "The load stayed within tolerance."

Toni flinched at the word tolerance.

Jayda caught the look. "You okay."

Toni hesitated. "I'm just... thinking."

"That's allowed," Jayda said lightly.

But Zee didn't miss the way Toni's fingers curled tighter around her notebook.

"The wind isn't nothing," Zee said. "It changes the variables."

Mikki exhaled. "It does. But it also doesn't automatically mean unsafe. Systems account for variance."

Jayda smiled at that. "See. Science again."

Zee didn't smile back. "Science also says you stop when conditions change."

Mikki shifted her weight. The yard felt smaller now, the space between the trees tighter somehow, like the air itself was listening. "We did stop," she said. "We observed."

"And then we tested," Jayda added.

Toni swallowed. *Testing isn't neutral*, she thought. *It's a choice.*

The wind brushed through again, softer this time. The rope barely moved.

Jayda pointed. "Look. It's calm now."

Zee followed the motion with her eyes. She hated how convincing it looked. "Calm doesn't mean stable."

"But it helps," Mikki said. "We don't need to shut everything down because of one shift."

Jayda stepped closer to the ladder without climbing it. "What if we just do one more," she said. "Not to push it. Just to confirm."

Zee stiffened. "Confirm what."

"That it still behaves," Jayda said. "Under the same conditions."

Toni finally spoke. "They're not the same conditions."

All three of them turned to her.

"The wind," Toni said, voice quieter but steady. "That changed. So it's not the same."

Jayda sighed. "I know. I just mean... same setup. Same rope. Same us."

Same us felt dangerous in a way Toni couldn't fully explain.

Mikki rubbed her thumb along the edge of her water bottle, thinking. "If we do another run," she said carefully, "we keep it conservative. No adjustments. No leaning. Straight path."

Jayda nodded immediately. "Straight. Promise."

Zee crossed her arms. "You promised that earlier too."

Jayda winced. "That wasn't—"

"I know," Zee said. "That's the problem."

The wind paused, as if waiting.

Mikki looked between them. She could feel the pull now, not just from the rope, but from the moment itself. Stopping felt like admitting fear. Continuing felt like proof.

"We're not doing this because it's fun," she said finally. "We're doing it because we need to understand what changed."

Toni's stomach tightened.

Understanding isn't the same as respecting, she thought.

But she still didn't say it.

Jayda looked relieved. "So... one more."

Zee hesitated, then nodded once. "One. And then we stop."

Jayda smiled. "Deal."

They moved into position with practiced ease.

Too much ease.

Zee checked the harness, slower than before, fingers lingering like she was trying to convince herself to feel something different. Mikki scanned the rope again, eyes tracing every familiar line. Toni stayed where she was, notebook pressed flat to her chest now, like she was bracing for something she couldn't name.

Jayda climbed the ladder.

Halfway up, she paused.

The wind lifted her hair and brushed across her face again, cooler this time.

"Still good," she called down.

Mikki raised her hand. "Straight run."

"Straight," Jayda echoed.

Zee took her position at the anchor, feet planted wider than necessary.

Toni held her breath.

Jayda stepped off.

The rope caught.

The pulley rolled.

The system did exactly what it had been doing all day.

For a moment, everything felt steady again.

And that was when the wind shifted once more.

Not stronger.

Just different.

Enough to remind them all that control was never as complete as it felt.

Still no fall.

But no one relaxed.

Not anymore.

Jayda landed clean.

The hay caught her the way it always did, soft and forgiving, dust lifting into the air before settling back down like nothing had happened. The rope steadied. The pulley slowed. The system completed its cycle.

On paper, it was a success.

Jayda sat up, brushing hay from her arms, breath coming a little faster than usual. "See," she said, smiling automatically. "Totally fine."

Mikki nodded. "The line recovered."

Zee didn't answer right away.

She stayed where she was, hands still on the rope, feeling the way it hummed beneath her palms. The vibration was faint now, almost gone, but she could still sense where it had traveled. The rope hadn't failed.

But it hadn't been quiet either.

Toni stepped forward without realizing she was moving. Her heart was beating too fast for a moment that had ended safely. That bothered her more than anything else.

"It sounded different," she said.

Jayda tilted her head. "Different how."

"I don't know," Toni admitted. "Just... different."

Mikki frowned slightly. "Sound changes with wind."

"And tension," Zee added. "And direction."

Jayda laughed once, sharp and quick. "Okay, but nothing broke."

Zee finally looked at her. "That's not the only measure."

The smile slid off Jayda's face, just a little. "You said one more. We did one more."

"And now we're done," Zee said.

Mikki nodded. "We stop here."

Jayda opened her mouth, then closed it again. She glanced back at the ladder, then at the rope, then at the space between the trees. Everything looked exactly the way it had before.

That was what made it hard.

"Does anyone else feel like it's lying," she asked.

"Lying," Mikki repeated.

Jayda shrugged. "Like... acting calm so you'll trust it."

Zee exhaled slowly. "Systems don't lie. People do."

Toni hugged her notebook closer to her chest. *Or people convince themselves,* she thought.

The wind passed through the yard again, gentler now, barely enough to move the leaves. The rope swayed once and then stilled.

"Pack it up," Zee said.

No one argued.

They worked in silence this time. The ladder went back to the shed. The rope was lowered and coiled, Zee looping it tighter than before, testing each turn even though it wasn't under load. Mikki watched every step, hands folded, committing the motions to memory. Jayda hovered nearby, quiet, letting the others take the lead without comment.

Toni didn't help.

She watched.

That felt like her job now.

When everything was put away, the yard looked ordinary again. Just grass. Just trees. Just late afternoon light stretching long across the ground.

Nothing broken.

Nothing wrong.

Nothing finished.

Jayda broke the silence first, softer than usual. "So... tomorrow."

Mikki didn't answer right away.

Zee did. "Tomorrow, we reassess."

Jayda nodded. "Before we run."

"Yes," Zee said. "Before anything."

Toni added, "Before it feels easy again."

That landed.

Mikki glanced at her, then nodded. "Before it feels normal."

The word normal hung there, heavier than it should have been.

They stood together for another moment, listening to the crickets start up again, the sound filling the space like static. The yard no longer felt inviting.

It felt alert.

As they turned toward the house, Toni looked back once more at the empty space between The Lookout and The Launch Tree.

Nothing was there.

But she could still see it.

And for the first time, the absence felt louder than the rope ever had.

Something changed today, she thought.

Even though nothing broke.

And that was the part that mattered.

Chapter 13
The Choice

The day after the wind passed felt almost kind.

Not bright in a dramatic way. Not heavy either. Just steady. The air moved when it was supposed to. Leaves stirred without scraping. The yard looked like a place where nothing urgent had ever happened.

That alone made Jayda suspicious, in a joking way.

"Well," she said, stepping off the porch and stretching her arms overhead, "if yesterday was the universe being dramatic, today feels like it's apologizing."

Mikki smiled despite herself. The numbers in her head lined up easily this morning. No pressure. No static. She liked days that behaved. "Weather systems correct," she said. "That's normal."

Zee didn't answer right away. She stood near the fence, eyes tracking the tops of the trees the way she always did now, watching for movement that wasn't there. The branches swayed gently, nothing more.

"Normal doesn't mean meaningless," she said finally.

Jayda waved a hand. "You sound like Toni."

Toni didn't look up from where she sat on the porch steps, notebook resting closed beside her. "I'll take that as a compliment," she said.

They lingered longer than they needed to, none of them in a hurry to do anything. The yard held its shape. The space between The Lookout and The Launch Tree looked ordinary again, empty in a way that no longer felt loud.

That should have felt like relief.

Mikki leaned against the porch railing, arms folded loosely. "We did the right thing yesterday," she said, not defensively. Just stating it. "We noticed. We stopped."

Jayda nodded. "See? Growth."

Zee glanced at her. "Stopping once doesn't make you careful forever."

Jayda grinned. "But it proves we can."

That landed quietly.

Toni felt it settle in her chest, that subtle shift where relief starts to feel like permission. She picked up her notebook, then set it back down without opening it.

The system didn't fail, she thought. That's not the same as being done.

A breeze moved through the yard, gentle enough to be pleasant. Leaves whispered. The grass bent and lifted again. Nothing creaked. Nothing warned.

Jayda rocked back on her heels. "I kind of like that it doesn't feel intense anymore," she said. "Like... we're past the hard part."

Mikki nodded slowly. "That's usually how progress feels."

Zee didn't nod.

Instead, she said, "That's usually how habits start."

Jayda laughed, light and easy. "You make everything sound ominous."

"I make things sound honest," Zee replied.

No one argued.

Toni watched the space between the trees again. Without the rope, it looked harmless. Smaller, even. Like something that had already been decided.

She didn't write that down.

Yet.

The morning stayed calm.

And in that calm, something else began to form.

They didn't mean to rebuild it that morning.

That was the story Mikki would have told later, if someone asked. No one said, Let's put it back up. No one named a plan. The idea arrived the way thoughts do when they've already been halfway agreed upon.

Zee was the one who broke the seal, though she didn't announce it.

She crossed the yard and crouched near the fence, fingers brushing the rope coil without lifting it. Just checking the weight. Just confirming it was still itself.

"It dried fine," she said.

Jayda looked up. "The rope?"

Zee nodded. "No stiffness. No fray."

Mikki straightened. "We weren't planning on using it today."

"I didn't say use," Zee replied. "I said check."

Jayda grinned. "Checking is basically your love language."

Zee snorted despite herself.

Toni felt it then. That subtle click inside her chest, like the moment a story decides its direction before the writer does. She picked up her notebook, not to write, but because holding it grounded her.

"Checking turns into setting," she said carefully.

Jayda glanced at her. "You're not wrong," she admitted. "But also... we're good at setting now."

Mikki hesitated.

That was new.

Yesterday, hesitation had felt sharp and necessary. Today, it felt almost rude, like slowing down a conversation everyone else was already having.

"We can set it without running it," she said finally. "Just to see if anything changed after the wind."

Zee looked up. "Exactly."

Jayda clapped her hands once. "Science field trip."

They moved with an ease that unsettled Toni more than yesterday's tension ever had. The ladder came out. The rope uncoiled smoothly. Zee looped it over the branch with practiced efficiency, hands steady, movements economical.

Too economical.

Mikki checked the angle by eye, then stopped herself. She reached for the tape measure, then paused again, fingers hovering.

Do we need it, she wondered.

The thought landed heavier than she expected.

She used it anyway.

Toni watched closely, tracking not the steps but the spaces between them. The moments where someone could have spoken and didn't. The places where a double check became a single glance.

Jayda noticed the silence first. "Okay, but can we admit this feels... fine?" she asked. "Like, nothing's pushing back."

Zee tightened the knot and tested it once. "Systems don't push back until they do."

Jayda rolled her shoulders. "You say that like it's personal."

"It is," Zee said quietly.

The rope hung clean between the trees, sunlight catching along its length. It looked right. It looked ready.

Toni's stomach tightened.

Ready for what, she wondered.

No one answered the question out loud, but they all stood there, staring at the same invisible possibility.

Mikki broke it. "We're not running it," she said. "We're just... deciding."

Jayda tilted her head. "Deciding what."

Mikki looked at the setup. The height. The line. The ground beneath it. Everything she knew said it would work.

Everything she felt said that wasn't the whole point.

"Deciding whether stopping yesterday was a pause," she said slowly, "or a rule."

That quieted Jayda.

Zee stood and brushed her hands on her shorts. "And if it's a pause," she said, "we need to say that out loud."

The breeze shifted again, light but noticeable, moving through the yard like it was listening.

Toni finally opened her notebook and wrote one line, neat and centered on the page.

This is where the choice lives.

She closed the book and waited.

The wind arrived without drama.

Not a gust. Not a warning. Just a steady breath moving through the yard, lifting the leaves enough to make the branches whisper to one another. The rope swayed slightly where it hung, a small motion that would have been easy to miss if they hadn't all been watching so closely.

Jayda noticed first. She always did.

"It's moving," she said.

Zee followed the line with her eyes. "Barely."

"Still moving," Jayda replied. "Yesterday it didn't do that."

Mikki crouched and pressed her palm flat against the ground beneath the line. The dirt was dry on top but looser underneath, powdery where feet had landed again and again. She rubbed her thumb against her fingers, feeling grit cling to her skin.

"The conditions are different," she said.

Jayda perked up. "Different doesn't mean bad."

"No," Mikki said. "It means new."

Zee shifted her weight, eyes flicking up to the branch. The leaves above it were stirring more now, not violently, but enough to keep the rope from fully settling. She reached out and steadied it with two fingers, then pulled her hand back like she'd touched something hot.

"That's the thing," she said. "It won't sit still."

Jayda crossed her arms. "Neither do we."

Toni felt the pull then. Not toward the rope exactly, but toward the moment itself. This was the part that always mattered. The place where facts stopped being enough and something else had to decide.

She opened her notebook.

The day doesn't have to be loud to change everything.

She underlined it once and closed the book again.

Mikki stood and wiped her hands on her shorts. "If we were running this today," she said carefully, "we'd have to adjust."

Jayda's eyes lit up. "Adjust how."

"Lower expectations," Mikki replied. "Shorter runs. More checks."

Zee added, "Or we don't run it at all."

The words landed between them, solid and unmoving.

Jayda looked from Zee to Mikki. "You're saying stop again."

"I'm saying choose again," Zee said.

Jayda exhaled sharply. "It feels like quitting."

"No," Mikki said. "It feels like deciding."

That gave Jayda pause.

She kicked lightly at the grass, then stilled herself. "What if we just test it," she said. "Not a full run. Just weight."

Zee frowned. "We already did that yesterday."

"Yesterday wasn't today," Jayda shot back. "You just said conditions changed."

Silence stretched.

The rope swayed again, the movement small but persistent, like it was refusing to be ignored.

Mikki closed her eyes for a second. She saw numbers line up, then slip. Saw how easily confidence smoothed over caution when nothing had gone wrong yet.

"We can test," she said slowly. "But only if we agree on what the test means."

Jayda nodded quickly. "Fine. What does it mean."

"It means," Mikki said, choosing each word, "that if anything feels off, we stop. No debate. No 'one more.'"

Zee looked at Jayda. "And stopping doesn't mean failure."

Jayda hesitated.

Just long enough.

"Okay," she said. "I can do that."

Toni watched her face, the way excitement and restraint pulled in opposite directions. This wasn't fear. This was want. And want was harder to manage.

They moved to set the weight, hands careful, movements slower than before. The rope dipped slightly as the bag was clipped on, the sway more noticeable now with the wind pressing against it.

Zee steadied the line. "Ready."

Mikki nodded. "Go."

They released.

The bag slid, the pulley humming low as it moved along the line. Halfway across, the rope dipped lower than it had yesterday, then recovered, the motion uneven but controlled.

Jayda let out a breath she hadn't realized she was holding. "See. Fine."

Zee didn't respond right away. She was watching the recovery, the way the rope didn't return to center immediately.

Mikki saw it too.

"It took longer," she said.

Jayda frowned. "Longer than what."

"Than it should have," Mikki replied.

The bag landed safely. Nothing broke. Nothing snapped. Nothing dramatic happened.

And somehow, that made it worse.

Toni wrote again, quickly this time.

Almost always sounds like nothing.

She closed the notebook and stepped closer to the others.

"So," Jayda said, forcing lightness into her voice. "What's the verdict."

Mikki looked at the rope.

At the wind.

At her friends.

"This," she said, "is where we decide if we're reacting to what happened yesterday… or paying attention to what could happen today."

No one spoke.

The rope swayed again, patient, waiting for them to choose.

No one moved right away.

The rope slowed, then stilled, then lifted again as the wind shifted direction. It was subtle enough that yesterday they would have ignored it. Today, it felt louder.

Jayda broke first. She always did when silence started to feel like pressure. "So what are we actually doing," she asked. "Because standing here pretending we're not thinking about it is worse than just saying it."

Zee folded her arms. "We're thinking about whether today is a build day or a no-build day."

Jayda scoffed. "It's always a build day."

"That's not true," Mikki said. Her voice wasn't sharp, but it carried weight. "Some days are check days. Some days are stop days."

Jayda turned to her. "Since when."

Mikki didn't answer immediately. She watched the rope instead, the way it tugged faintly against the branch. "Since we realized systems don't care what day it is."

That landed.

Jayda's jaw tightened. "You're talking like this thing has a personality."

Zee shook her head. "No. We're talking like it has conditions."

Toni stepped closer, notebook tucked against her side. She hadn't written since the test, but the words were still stacking up in her head, lining themselves into sentences whether she invited them or not.

"This feels like the part," she said quietly.

All three of them looked at her.

"The part where stories split," Toni continued. "Not because something big happens. But because people decide what they're going to listen to."

Jayda crossed her arms. "And what are we listening to."

"The wind," Zee said immediately.

"The data," Mikki said at the same time.

Jayda threw up her hands. "Okay, see, this is what I mean. You both sound right and also impossible."

Mikki turned toward her fully now. "What do you want to do."

Jayda opened her mouth, then stopped. She hadn't expected the question to come that cleanly. No arguing. No warnings. Just choice.

"I want to run it," she said finally. "I want to feel it again. But I don't want to be stupid about it."

Zee nodded once. "That matters."

"It does," Mikki agreed. "But wanting it doesn't make it neutral."

Jayda exhaled hard. "Nothing ever is."

Toni opened her notebook again. She didn't sit. She didn't lean. She stood right there in the grass and wrote.

Want doesn't disappear just because you understand it.

She underlined it twice.

Zee watched her write, then looked back at Jayda. "If we do this," she said, "we're choosing to accept whatever the conditions bring. No pretending later that we didn't see them."

Jayda met her gaze. "I see them."

Mikki stepped in. "And we're choosing not to frame it as an accident if something goes wrong."

That made Jayda flinch.

"What does that mean," she asked.

"It means," Mikki said slowly, "that we own the decision. Before. Not after."

The wind picked up just enough to rustle the leaves harder now, branches creaking faintly. The rope shifted again, brushing bark with a quiet scrape.

Toni closed her notebook.

"This is the choice chapter," she said, almost to herself.

Jayda laughed weakly. "Of course you'd say that."

"No," Toni replied. "I'm writing it down so I don't lie to myself later."

Silence again. Thicker this time.

Zee finally spoke. "If we stop today, nothing bad happens."

Jayda nodded. "And if we don't."

"Nothing bad has to happen," Mikki said. "But something could."

Jayda stared at the rope, then at the space beneath it. The grass there was flattened in places, darker where the dirt showed through. Evidence of yesterday. Proof that wanting had already left marks.

She rubbed her palms together, grounding herself. "I don't want to stop just because I'm scared."

Zee's voice softened. "Sometimes stopping isn't fear. It's accuracy."

Jayda looked at her. "And sometimes stopping is pretending you don't trust yourself."

That one hit harder.

Mikki swallowed. This was the edge. She could feel it. The place where logic stopped being enough and belief stepped in.

"So what do we trust more," Mikki asked quietly. "Ourselves, or the rules we made when we were thinking clearly."

The wind answered first, pushing the rope into motion again.

Toni felt it in her chest, the moment locking into place. Whatever happened next would belong to them.

Not to chance.

Not to luck.

To choice.

She wrote one last line before snapping the notebook shut.

This is where we decide what we are responsible for.

They all stood there, the yard holding its breath, waiting for someone to say yes.

Or no.

No one spoke at first.

The wind eased, then returned, uneven now. Not strong. Just inconsistent. Enough to keep the rope from settling completely still.

Jayda broke the quiet with a breathy laugh that wasn't really laughter. "I hate this part," she said. "Where everyone's being careful and I can feel myself wanting to be brave just to prove something."

Zee shook her head. "Bravery isn't proving. It's choosing what you're willing to carry after."

Jayda looked at her. "And what are you willing to carry."

Zee answered without hesitation. "That we stopped when the conditions changed."

Mikki felt that answer land somewhere deep. She turned to Jayda. "If we go again today, we're saying the wind doesn't get a vote."

Jayda frowned. "I don't like thinking of it that way."

"That's because it takes control away," Mikki said. "And control is comforting."

Toni stepped forward, surprising herself. "But control is also the illusion that gets people hurt."

All eyes shifted to her.

She didn't back down.

"We didn't almost mess up because we didn't know enough," Toni continued. "We almost messed up because we trusted the system more than the moment."

Jayda closed her eyes briefly. When she opened them, something had settled.

"So if we stop," she said, "it's not because we're afraid."

"No," Zee said. "It's because today is a different day."

Mikki nodded. "Different inputs. Different call."

Jayda stared at the rope one last time. She imagined the feel of it. The rush. The clean arc through the air. She imagined the way it had shuddered earlier, just once.

Then she stepped back.

"Okay," she said. "We stop."

The word did not wobble.

It felt solid.

Mikki released a breath she hadn't realized she'd been holding. Zee moved immediately, efficient and calm, beginning the process of securing everything without ceremony. Not rushed. Not dramatic. Just done right.

Toni watched them work and didn't write.

This part didn't need ink yet.

When the rope was fully stowed and the ladder carried away, the yard looked plain again. Trees. Grass. Wind moving through leaves like it always had.

Jayda stood with her hands on her hips. "I don't like that this feels harder than running it."

Zee gave a small smile. "That's how you know it mattered."

Mikki added quietly, "This is the decision that makes the next one possible."

Jayda nodded once. "Then tomorrow we decide again."

The wind moved through the trees one more time, softer now.

The yard exhaled.

And without announcing it, without promising anything out loud, they stepped away together, carrying the weight of the choice they had just made.

Not relieved.

Not disappointed.

Responsible.

That was new.

And it would matter later.

Chapter 14
The Fall

The first thing Toni noticed was the wind.

Not that it was strong. Not that it was loud. Just that it was doing something she hadn't seen it do before.

It slid sideways through the yard instead of straight across, brushing the tops of the grass and then lifting, uneven, like it couldn't decide where it wanted to go. Leaves rattled against each other without rhythm. The air touched Toni's arms and then pulled away again, cool and insistent, like someone testing a door that wasn't meant to open yet.

She paused at the edge of the porch.

No one else stopped.

Jayda was already clipping in, movements easy and practiced, like her body knew this part better than her mind did. Zee stood near the anchor, hands loose at her sides, eyes tracking the rope the way they always did. Mikki hovered a step back, watching the setup without counting this time, her attention spread thin and wide instead of sharp and focused.

Everything looked right.

That was the problem.

The rope hung between The Lookout and The Launch Tree with the same familiar line it always made, clean and confident against the bark. The pulley sat where it should. The ladder hadn't shifted. The knots hadn't moved. Nothing was wrong in any way Toni could name.

Still, her stomach tightened.

She adjusted her grip on her phone, thumb hovering near the screen without pressing record. She hadn't planned to film this run. She wasn't sure why she'd even brought it out. Habit, maybe. Or instinct. Or the quiet sense that something should be held onto, just in case.

Just in case of what? she asked herself.

She didn't have an answer.

Jayda laughed at something Mikki said, the sound bright and unbothered. Zee glanced up once at the trees, then back to the rope. Mikki raised her hand halfway, then lowered it again, like the signal wasn't necessary anymore.

"Ready?" Jayda called.

The word sounded different today. Less like a question. More like a formality.

Toni opened her mouth, then closed it again.

What would she even say?

The wind feels wrong?

The air is acting strange?

I have a feeling?

Feelings didn't count as data. She knew that. Mikki had taught her that, without ever meaning to.

Jayda stepped onto the platform.

The breeze shifted again, tugging at Jayda's shirt, lifting the ends of her braids for just a second before letting them fall. The rope gave a small, almost imperceptible sway, then settled.

Toni's chest felt tight.

Not fear. Not yet.

Something closer to recognition.

She lowered the phone slightly, eyes locked on the line, watching the space around it instead of the rope itself. The air there seemed thicker somehow, like it was waiting to be disturbed.

Jayda leaned forward, weight transferring, muscles trusting what they had trusted every time before.

"Three," Mikki said, her voice steady.

The wind brushed Toni's cheek again, sharper now.

Something's different, Toni thought.

Not dangerous.

Not broken.

Just... off.

"Two."

The leaves overhead shivered, though the branches didn't move.

Toni's fingers curled tight around the phone.

"One."

Jayda stepped into motion.

And for the smallest possible moment, everything still made sense.

Jayda left the platform the way she always did.

Confident. Centered. Like gravity was something she had already negotiated with.

The pulley caught clean, rolling forward with a familiar hum as her weight transferred fully onto the line. For half a second, the motion followed the pattern they all knew by heart. The arc. The speed. The way her body settled into the ride like it belonged there.

Toni's breath loosened just a little.

Then the wind pushed.

Not hard. Not violently. Just enough to matter.

It slid across the line instead of past it, pressing sideways, changing the way the rope held tension. The pulley answered with a sound Toni hadn't heard before. Not a squeal. Not a snap. Something lower. A strained, unfamiliar vibration that traveled through the rope and into the air around it.

Zee felt it first.

Her head snapped up, body reacting before thought could catch up. Her hands lifted instinctively, fingers spreading like she could steady the system by force of will alone.

"That's not right," she said.

Jayda felt it next.

The ride shifted beneath her, the smooth glide breaking into something uneven. Her stomach dropped harder than it should have, the rhythm changing just enough to steal the laugh from her throat.

"Hey," she said, more surprised than scared.

Mikki stepped forward at the same moment, heart slamming. Her eyes tracked the line, the anchor point, the angle. Everything she had trusted was still there. Still holding. Still within limits.

But the limits were moving.

The rope dipped lower than it ever had before.

Not dramatically. Not enough to scream yet.

Enough to notice.

Toni's thumb hit the screen.

The red light blinked on, capturing motion without meaning to, her hands shaking so badly the frame wobbled. She didn't lower the phone. She couldn't look away.

Jayda tightened her grip, muscles tensing as she tried to correct her balance midair. The pulley stuttered, caught, then lurched forward again.

The wind gusted a second time.

Stronger now.

The rope shuddered.

Zee shouted Jayda's name.

Mikki opened her mouth to say something, anything, but the sound never made it out.

The system didn't fail all at once.

It hesitated.

That was worse.

The line twisted just enough to throw the pulley off its clean track. There was a sharp crack, like wood snapping under too much weight, followed by a sound that Toni would later recognize as fibers tearing, one after another, fast and violent.

The rope recoiled.

Not away.

Down.

Jayda's body jerked sideways, momentum no longer controlled, no longer guided. The air rushed out of her lungs in a sharp, startled sound that barely counted as a scream.

For one impossible heartbeat, she was suspended between directions.

Then the line gave way completely.

The sound that followed was not loud at first.

It was sudden.

And then everything else came apart.

The rope snapped like a decision made too late.

The recoil flung Jayda sideways, not down the path they had measured and trusted, but off it entirely. Her body spun, weight no longer centered, no longer supported. The pulley tore free with a metallic shriek and disappeared into the trees, leaves exploding outward as something heavy slammed through them.

Toni screamed.

She did not remember choosing to. The sound ripped out of her chest, sharp and raw, her hands still locked around the phone as the image blurred into streaks of green and sky and panic.

Jayda hit the branches first.

They cracked and split under her weight, slowing her just enough to make the fall last longer. Each impact jolted her body in a new direction, pain flashing white-hot and then vanishing beneath the next blow. Her braids caught and snapped free, beads scattering like thrown pebbles.

Mikki was already moving.

Her clipboard hit the platform and slid uselessly across the wood as she lunged forward, hands outstretched toward empty air. She did not make a sound. Her mouth was open, but nothing came out. Her brain refused to accept the space where Jayda should have been.

Zee ran.

She did not think. She did not hesitate. Her feet left the ground as she launched herself down the ladder two rungs at a time, boots slipping, hands scraping bark as she hit the dirt and kept going. Branches whipped against her arms and face, but she didn't slow.

Jayda's body struck the ground with a sound that did not belong in the woods.

A heavy, final thud.

Then nothing.

No laughter.

No shouting.

No movement.

The world went quiet in a way that felt wrong.

Toni's phone slipped from her fingers and hit the ground face down, the recording still running somewhere no one was watching. Her legs locked, refusing to move, her chest tight and burning as she tried to breathe.

Mikki dropped to her knees at the edge of the platform.

The distance between where she was and where Jayda lay felt impossible. Too far. Too sudden. She stared into the space, eyes wide, mind racing backward through measurements and angles and knots, searching for the moment she should have stopped this.

This is not how it ends, she thought.

This is not how it goes.

Zee reached Jayda first.

She skidded to a stop beside her, dropping hard onto her knees, hands hovering inches above Jayda's body as she forced herself not to touch anything yet. Jayda lay twisted against the dirt, one arm bent wrong beneath her, chest rising and falling in short, uneven bursts.

"Jayda," Zee said, her voice low and steady despite the way her heart hammered. "Do not move. Okay? Do not move."

Jayda's eyes fluttered open.

For a terrifying second, they didn't focus.

Then she sucked in a shaky breath and whispered, "It hurts."

The sound shattered whatever was left holding them together.

Mikki slid down the ladder and ran, shoes slipping in the dirt as she crossed the clearing. She dropped beside Jayda, hands trembling as she tried to decide where she could touch without making things worse.

"I am so sorry," she said, the words tumbling out before she could stop them. "I checked it. I checked everything."

Toni finally moved.

Her feet carried her forward without permission, legs shaking so badly she nearly fell. Tears blurred everything into streaks of brown and green and sky. She stopped a few steps away, frozen, eyes cataloging details she did not want to see. The scrape along Jayda's arm. The dirt pressed flat beneath her body. The way the rope's loose end swayed above them, frayed and useless.

Zee reached for the first aid kit strapped to her back.

Just in case.

She had packed it that morning without explaining why.

Now her hands moved fast and precise, muscle memory taking over as fear threatened to swallow her whole.

"Toni," Zee said sharply. "Go get help. Now."

Toni didn't move.

The woods felt too big. Too quiet. Her ears rang as if the world were underwater.

"Toni," Zee said again, louder this time. "Run."

That broke through.

Toni turned and ran, sandals slapping against dirt and roots, lungs burning as branches tore at her arms. She did not look back. She could not. The sound of Jayda's uneven breathing followed her like a countdown she didn't understand.

Behind her, the zipline creaked softly in the breeze.

Ahead of her, everything was already changing.

Time fractured.

Not all at once. Not cleanly. It stretched thin in places and snapped in others, moments dragging until they felt unreal, then vanishing entirely as if they had never happened.

Zee stayed with Jayda.

Her hands finally settled, careful and deliberate. She checked Jayda's breathing first. Short. Uneven. Still there. Zee counted silently, anchoring herself to the rhythm because counting was something she could do. Something solid.

"Stay with me," she said quietly. "Just breathe. You're doing great."

Jayda nodded, a small, jerky movement that made Zee tense. "Okay," Jayda whispered, like she was agreeing to a rule she didn't fully understand.

Mikki hovered on the other side, knees pressed into the dirt, palms flat against the ground like she needed to feel something stable. Her thoughts chased each other in circles.

The angle was right.
The load was within limits.
We reset the anchor.

She tried to line the facts up the way she always did, but they refused to stay still. Each one slid out of place the moment she touched it.

"This is my fault," she said, the words spilling out in a rush she couldn't stop. "I should have stopped it. I should have called it earlier."

Zee didn't look at her. "Not now," she said firmly. "You can think about that later."

"But the measurements," Mikki insisted, voice breaking. "The rope shouldn't have snapped. It shouldn't have—"

"It did," Zee said. Not harsh. Just final. "We deal with what's happening, not what shouldn't have."

Jayda squeezed her eyes shut. "Can you stop arguing," she murmured. "My head feels weird."

That did it.

Mikki swallowed hard and nodded, even though her throat felt too tight to move. "I'm here," she said, softer now. "I'm not going anywhere."

The woods felt closer than they had before. Branches pressed in, leaves whispering overhead like they were talking about them. The broken rope swayed above, catching the light, each movement small but impossible to ignore.

Zee followed protocol without calling it that.

She checked Jayda's pupils. She checked for bleeding. She kept her hands visible and still, her voice low and steady. The first aid kit lay open beside her, supplies lined up neatly even though she had not used them yet.

Preparedness was not the same as readiness.

Jayda shifted and gasped, a sharp sound that cut straight through Zee's chest. Zee's hands lifted instinctively, then froze again.

"Don't move," Zee said gently. "I know it hurts. I know. Help is coming."

Jayda's eyes flicked toward Mikki. "You okay," she asked.

The question felt wrong. Upside down. Mikki let out a shaky breath that might have been a laugh if it didn't sound so broken.

"I'm fine," she lied. "You just focus on you."

Jayda nodded, satisfied enough with that.

The sound came faint at first.

A distant wail, barely there, carried on the wind.

Sirens.

Zee felt her shoulders drop just a fraction. Relief threaded through her chest, sharp and painful.

"They're coming," she said. "You hear that? That's for you."

Jayda's lips twitched. "Told you," she whispered. "Crash Queen."

"Do not joke," Mikki said quickly, then immediately softened. "Please."

Jayda smiled anyway, a small, tired curve of her mouth. "I'm serious," she said. "Guess I lived up to the name."

The sirens grew louder.

Footsteps echoed in the distance. Voices. Someone calling out, urgent and sharp. The world began to move again, sound rushing back in all at once. Birds scattered. Leaves shook. The woods let go of its breath.

Zee finally looked up.

Adults were coming through the trees, moving fast, faces already tight with fear and questions. The moment stretched, fragile and final, balanced between before and after.

Zee pressed her hand lightly against Jayda's shoulder, grounding both of them. "You did nothing wrong," she said, not as comfort, but as instruction. "Just stay still."

Jayda nodded again.

Above them, the rope hung useless and quiet.

Below it, everything had changed.

The adults arrived in pieces.

First voices. Then shapes moving too fast through the trees. Then hands that didn't belong to any of them, reaching in careful, practiced ways. Someone asked questions that blurred together. Someone else answered with words that felt wrong in their mouths.

Zee stepped back when she was told to, even though every part of her resisted it. Her hands curled into fists at her sides, empty now, like she had been cut loose from something important.

Mikki stood when someone touched her shoulder and immediately wished she hadn't. The ground tilted beneath her feet, the world narrowing to sound and motion she couldn't quite keep up with. She leaned hard against a tree trunk until it stopped spinning.

Toni stayed where she was.

She hadn't realized she'd dropped to her knees until she tried to stand and couldn't. The notebook lay open beside her in the dirt, pages fluttering in the breeze. She didn't look at it. She couldn't. Writing would turn this into something shaped, something finished.

This wasn't finished.

A paramedic knelt beside Jayda, voice calm, steady, asking her questions that sounded too ordinary for what had just happened.

"Can you tell me your name."

"Do you know where you are."

"Does it hurt anywhere else."

Jayda answered all of them.

Her voice was quieter now, but it was there. That mattered more than anything.

Zee watched the way the paramedic's hands moved, efficient and sure. She cataloged each step automatically, the way she always did. Stabilize. Assess. Protect. Control what you can.

There was a stretcher.

That was when it became real in a new way.

Jayda looked suddenly small against the bright orange frame, straps waiting to be pulled tight. She noticed it too.

"Hey," she said, eyes flicking toward Mikki. "You're not coming with me?"

The question landed hard.

Mikki stepped forward without thinking. "I am," she said. "I'm right here."

A hand stopped her gently. "We've got her," a voice said. "You can follow."

Follow.

Not fix. Not undo. Just follow.

Zee moved closer again, careful not to be in the way. She met Jayda's eyes and held them. "You're doing great," she said. "Just like always."

Jayda tried to smile. It didn't quite work, but it was close enough.

Toni finally stood.

Her legs shook, but she forced them to hold. She stepped closer too, close enough that Jayda could see her.

"I'm sorry," Toni said, the words coming out thin and fragile. "I didn't—"

Jayda cut her off. "Don't," she said softly. "You ran. That was the right thing."

Toni nodded, tears finally spilling over. She wiped them away with the back of her hand, angry at herself for shaking.

The stretcher lifted.

The woods seemed to recoil as Jayda was carried through them, branches bending back, leaves brushing her shoes like they were trying to say goodbye. The rope above stayed where it was, broken end swaying gently, completely indifferent.

That hurt more than anything else.

Mikki couldn't stop staring at it.

Zee noticed and stepped in front of her line of sight, just slightly. Not blocking it completely. Just enough.

"Later," Zee said quietly. "We deal with that later."

Mikki nodded, grateful she didn't have to argue.

When Jayda disappeared past the tree line, the space she left behind felt wrong. Too open. Too empty. Like a sound that had been cut off mid-note.

The yard filled with adults now. Questions layered over each other. Explanations tried and abandoned. Someone mentioned calling parents. Someone else said the word accident like it was supposed to make sense of everything.

It didn't.

Toni closed her notebook.

Not because she was done.

Because she understood something new.

This was the part you couldn't write your way out of.

The rope hung useless above them. The ladder lay on its side where it had been knocked over, forgotten. The hay was disturbed, marked with the shape of a body that had landed where it shouldn't have.

Almost had passed.

This was after.

And none of them were the same girls who had started the morning believing systems only failed when you ignored them.

Sometimes, they learned, systems failed the moment you trusted them too much.

The sirens faded down the road.

What remained was silence.

Heavy. Earned. Unavoidable.

This was the fall.

And now they would have to live with it.

Chapter 15
What We Found in the Fall

The house sounded wrong.

The clock on the wall did not tick the way it usually did. Each second landed too hard, too sharp, like it was trying to force itself into a space that no longer fit it.

Tick.

Tick.

Tick.

The sound was even, but it felt uneven, pressing instead of passing. Toni found herself counting without meaning to, waiting for one of the seconds to soften. None of them did.

A car passed outside, tires hissing against the road, close enough to hear and then already gone. The sound left a hollow behind it, like the house had inhaled and forgotten to breathe out.

Somewhere deeper in the house, Grandma Dot moved around the kitchen. A cabinet opened. A dish touched another dish. Not loud. Not careless. Just the small, ordinary clink of porcelain settling into place. The noise grounded everything and made it worse at the same time. The world was still doing what it always did.

The living room looked the same as it had that morning. Shoes by the door. The couch pillows slightly crooked. Jayda's hoodie still draped over the armrest where she had tossed it earlier, one sleeve hanging down like it was reaching for something.

No one sat there.

Mikki stood near the center of the room, not leaning on anything, not trusting her legs enough to move. The space felt crowded even though it was empty. Every object seemed louder than it should have been. The table. The lamp. The corner where the light from the window cut across the floor in a clean rectangle that did not belong to this moment.

Zee sat on the floor with her back against the couch, knees pulled up, hands resting flat on the carpet like she was anchoring herself. She stared straight ahead, not at the TV, not at the window, but at the place between them where nothing was happening.

Toni stood near the doorway, half in and half out of the room, notebook pressed under her arm. She did not take it out. She did not open it. Writing would make this real in a way she could not control yet.

The clock kept going.

Tick.

Tick.

Tick.

Each sound felt like a reminder they had not asked for.

No one spoke. Not because there was nothing to say. Because whatever came next would matter, and none of them knew how to carry it yet.

The house held them anyway.

Not gently.

Just firmly enough that they did not fall apart.

The space Jayda usually took up was too quiet.

It wasn't just that she wasn't there. It was that everything else kept adjusting around the place she should have been, like the room hadn't caught up yet. The couch cushion stayed slightly indented where she always dropped first. The arm of the chair looked unfinished without her sneaker hooked over it. Even the air felt wrong, stretched thin where her voice usually lived.

Mikki noticed it when she shifted her weight and expected someone to complain.

Jayda always complained when people blocked the middle of the room. About traffic flow. About bad design. About how standing in doorways was a crime against common sense. The comment didn't come, and Mikki's stomach tightened as if she'd missed a step.

She moved instead, slow and deliberate, setting Jayda's hoodie more neatly on the couch. The fabric was still warm, like it remembered her body. Mikki's hands stilled there longer than necessary.

"I didn't even hear it," she said suddenly.

The words came out flat, unplanned.

Zee's head tilted slightly. "Hear what."

"The rope," Mikki said. "I didn't hear it change. It just... did."

The silence after that was heavier than before.

Zee pressed her palms harder into the carpet. She could still feel the vibration in her hands if she thought about it long enough. The shudder. The way the tension had spoken without warning. She had trusted the rope because it had always answered her before.

"I felt it," she said. "But not soon enough."

Toni shifted in the doorway, the notebook sliding slightly against her ribs. "I wrote almost," she said quietly. "Before it happened. I didn't know why."

No one looked at her like she was strange.

That mattered.

Mikki's jaw tightened. "Almost isn't a measurement," she said. "You can't plan for it. You can't calculate it."

"But it still tells you something," Toni replied. Her voice was steadier than she expected it to be. "It tells you where the edge is."

Zee closed her eyes briefly. When she opened them again, her gaze went to the window, to the line of trees beyond the yard. "Edges don't announce themselves," she said. "They wait."

The clock kept ticking.

Tick.

Tick.

Mikki rubbed her hands together, then stopped when she realized she was doing it. "I keep replaying the order," she said. "What we checked. What we skipped. The sequence mattered. I know it did."

Zee nodded once. "We shortened it."

Mikki swallowed. "We trusted it."

Toni stepped fully into the room then, the doorway releasing her. "You're allowed to trust things," she said. "You just can't stop watching them."

That landed differently.

Zee leaned her head back against the couch, staring up at the ceiling. "I didn't tell her to stop," she said. "When she touched the rope. I should have."

"You did tell her," Mikki said. "Just... later."

Later felt cruel now.

Outside, another car passed, slower this time, the sound lingering longer before fading. Somewhere in the kitchen, Grandma Dot set something down gently, as if she knew sharp sounds wouldn't be welcome right now.

The house kept making room for them.

Toni finally slid down the wall and sat on the floor, pulling her notebook into her lap without opening it. "We're not bad people," she said, not asking.

"No," Zee said immediately.

Mikki nodded. "But we made a choice."

The word sat between them, solid and unavoidable.

Choice meant agency.

Agency meant responsibility.

The clock marked another second.

Tick.

And for the first time since they'd come inside, all three of them understood the same thing at once.

This wasn't the part where they figured out what went wrong.

This was the part where they learned what it meant that something had.

Night arrived without asking.

The light in the living room dimmed slowly, shadows stretching until they blurred the edges of everything. The corner where the wall met the ceiling darkened first, then the space beneath the table, then the hallway that led toward the bedrooms. No one reached for a lamp. It felt wrong to decide the lighting when nothing else felt decided yet.

Zee was the one who stood up.

Not suddenly. Not dramatically. Just enough to remind them that bodies still had weight and gravity still worked. She crossed to the window and pushed it open a few inches. The screen rattled softly before settling.

Air moved in.

It smelled like grass and late summer and something damp from the trees. It was the same air they had been breathing all day, but it felt different now. Cooler. Less forgiving.

Mikki followed the sound with her eyes. "The wind's changed," she said.

Zee nodded. "It does that at night."

Toni watched the curtain lift and fall, lift and fall, like the house itself was breathing. "It feels like it started earlier," she said. "Like it didn't wait."

No one corrected her.

Mikki sank onto the edge of the couch at last, elbows braced on her knees. Her shoulders looked smaller like that, folded inward instead of squared. "I keep thinking about how fast it became normal," she said. "How fast we stopped being careful."

Zee didn't turn from the window. "Normal is the most dangerous setting," she said. "It's where alarms go quiet."

Toni pressed her thumb into the notebook's cover, tracing the faint crease there from being opened and closed too many times. "When something works," she said slowly, "people start believing it will keep working just because it has."

Mikki let out a breath that trembled at the end. "I believed that."

"So did I," Zee said.

The admission hung there, unprotected.

Outside, a branch scraped lightly against the side of the house, a dry, dragging sound that made Toni flinch before she caught herself. Zee reached out and steadied the window, pulling it in another inch until the noise stopped.

"That sound," Toni said. "It's like when the rope moved."

Zee's hand stilled. "Yeah," she said. "Like something asking if you're paying attention."

Silence settled again, but it was a different kind now. Less frozen. More aware.

Mikki rubbed at her face, then dropped her hands to her lap. "We didn't fall because we were reckless," she said. "We fell because we were comfortable."

Toni nodded. "Comfort feels earned. That's why it's convincing."

Zee finally turned back toward them. Her eyes were steady, but tired. "So what did we find," she asked, "when everything dropped out from under us."

The question wasn't rhetorical.

Mikki thought first. Then spoke. "That systems don't fail loudly at the beginning," she said. "They fail quietly. In inches. In almosts."

Toni added, "That noticing is a responsibility, not a personality trait."

Zee leaned back against the wall, folding her arms loosely. "And that stopping isn't the same as quitting," she said. "Sometimes it's the only thing holding everything together."

The clock marked another second.

Tick.

This time, it didn't feel like an accusation.

It felt like a marker.

They sat with that, the three of them, as the night finished settling into place around the house. Outside, the wind moved through the trees again, steady now, not sudden. Inside, nothing was fixed.

But something had been named.

And naming it changed the shape of the room.

They did not stay frozen forever.

It happened slowly, the way ice loosens its grip without making a sound. Zee shifted first, uncurling her fingers from the carpet one at a time. The fibers clung briefly to her skin, then let go. She rubbed her palms together, not for warmth, but to feel something solid respond.

Mikki moved next. She crossed the room and sat on the edge of the chair instead of the couch, choosing the harder surface without thinking. Her posture stayed upright, precise, like she was still bracing for impact. She rested her hands on her knees and stared at them, as if expecting to see evidence there. Scratches. Dirt. Something she could measure.

There was nothing.

Toni finally stepped fully into the room. The doorway released her like it had been holding its breath. She sat on the floor near Zee, close enough that their shoulders almost touched but didn't. The notebook stayed under her arm, closed and firm, like a promise she wasn't ready to make.

Outside, a breeze moved through the trees. The sound filtered in faintly through the open window, leaves brushing against each other in a way that would have felt peaceful any other day. Now it just felt distant.

Zee broke the silence. Her voice came out low and even, practiced calm settling over it like a second skin. "We should talk about what almost happened."

Jayda's name stayed unspoken between them.

Mikki nodded once. "Not later," she said. "Now."

That mattered.

Toni felt it settle into the room, that choice. Talking now meant not letting the moment shrink into something harmless in memory. It meant holding it at its real size.

Zee exhaled slowly. "When the ladder shifted," she said, "my body reacted before my brain did. That's not a good thing or a bad thing. It's just information."

Mikki looked up. "What kind."

"That we were already too comfortable."

The words landed without accusation. They didn't need one.

Mikki swallowed. "I thought comfort meant we'd done it right."

"Comfort means repetition," Zee said. "Not safety."

Toni nodded without realizing she was doing it. She could still feel the way the moment had stretched, thin and sharp, when the ladder rocked. The way her breath had disappeared completely for half a second.

"Almost feels quiet afterward," she said. "Like it tries to pretend it didn't matter."

Zee looked at her. "But it does."

"Yes," Toni said. "That's the problem."

The clock ticked again, steady and insistent.

Tick.

Mikki flinched this time. She didn't hide it.

"I keep thinking about how close it was," she said. "Not to breaking. To us not noticing."

Zee leaned her head back against the couch. "That's usually where things go wrong."

No one rushed to fill the space after that. They let the words sit, heavy but necessary. The room felt altered now, not fragile, but reconfigured. Like furniture moved after something important had happened.

Toni finally slid the notebook from under her arm and set it on the floor between them. She didn't open it. She just placed it there, a shared center point.

"This," she said softly, "is the part people skip when they tell stories later."

Mikki glanced at it. "The thinking part."

"The noticing part," Zee corrected.

They all sat with that.

The house continued around them. The kitchen hummed faintly. The outside world kept passing. But inside the living room, something had shifted into place, solid and deliberate.

Not fear.

Attention.

And once it was there, none of them could pretend they hadn't felt it.

They did not decide anything that night.

That, Toni realized later, mattered just as much as the things they did say.

The conversation loosened, not because it was finished, but because it had reached the edge of what they could hold all at once. Zee stood and crossed to the window, resting her forehead briefly against the glass. Mikki leaned back in the chair, spine finally giving an inch, shoulders dropping like she had set something down without realizing she'd been carrying it. Toni picked up the notebook again and tucked it back under her arm, not to hide it, just to keep it close.

Outside, the last of the daylight thinned into blue. The yard darkened in layers, the trees turning into outlines instead of details. The space between The Lookout and The Launch Tree disappeared into shadow, indistinct and quiet.

Jayda wasn't there to fill it.

The absence pressed in gently at first, then harder when no one spoke her name. Toni felt it in her chest, a hollow that didn't ache yet but promised it might.

Zee broke the silence with a question that surprised them all. "Do you think," she said, still facing the window, "that we would've stopped if it hadn't almost happened."

Mikki didn't answer right away. She watched the slow turn of the ceiling fan, the way the blades blurred into something softer than motion. "I want to say yes," she said finally. "But I don't know if that's true."

Toni nodded. "I don't either."

That honesty felt like another small thing found in the fall. Not blame. Not certainty. Just truth.

Zee turned back to them. "Then that's what we take with us," she said. "Not what we meant to do. What we almost didn't."

The clock marked another second.

Tick.

This time, it didn't feel as sharp.

They stood eventually, one by one, moving through the room with careful normalcy. Lights were turned on. A blanket was folded. Someone straightened the pillows without thinking. The house accepted the motions, held them in place.

At the doorway, Toni paused. She looked back at the room, at the empty space where they had sat together, at the notebook tucked under her arm like a quiet witness.

We didn't just lose something, she thought. *We learned where it lived.*

She didn't write that down.

Not yet.

The night closed in around the house, steady and patient. Somewhere beyond the walls, the world kept going. And inside, without naming it, they carried forward the same understanding.

The fall hadn't taken everything.

It had shown them what mattered enough to hold onto.

Chapter 16
Telling the Truth

No one said it right away.

They sat where they had settled after everything else stopped moving, bodies angled toward one another without quite touching, like proximity itself carried weight now. Enough time had passed for the house to find its rhythm again, though it still felt careful, as if it remembered what had happened and did not want to rush them past it.

Late summer pressed in softly. The light slanted lower than it used to. Cicadas still hummed, but not with the same insistence. Outside, a lawn mower started somewhere down the block and faded again.

Jayda rested her hands in her lap, fingers twisting the edge of her sleeve until the fabric stretched thin. Her cast was still there, heavy and white, a solid reminder she could not negotiate with. Sitting upright felt possible again, even if standing too long did not. Healing had its own rules.

Zee leaned back against the porch railing, arms crossed, eyes fixed on the yard like she could still see the line there if she concentrated hard enough. Toni sat on the step below them, notebook closed beside her knee for once, her palms flat on the wood.

Mikki stood.

She hadn't meant to. Her legs just straightened, like they had decided something before the rest of her did. She took one step, then stopped, realizing she had everyone's attention.

"We can't just... not say anything," she said.

The words landed quietly. Not sharp. Not dramatic. Just true.

Jayda didn't look up. "Say what," she asked, though they all knew.

"The whole thing," Mikki said. "Not the safe version. Not the part that sounds better after you tell it a few times."

Zee exhaled through her nose. "You mean the part where we bent rules."

"The part where we made choices," Mikki said. "And kept making them."

Silence stretched again, thinner this time. Toni felt it pull tight in her chest, the way it always did when something important hovered just out of reach.

Jayda finally lifted her head. Her eyes moved between their faces, searching, weighing. "Are we talking about telling an adult," she said.

"Yes," Zee said, without hesitation.

Jayda swallowed. "Like... actually telling."

"Actually telling," Mikki confirmed.

No one rushed to soften it. No one said *it'll be fine* or *we didn't mean to* or *nothing really happened*. The absence of those words mattered.

Toni shifted closer, knees brushing Jayda's. "If we don't tell it," she said quietly, "it turns into something else."

"What," Jayda asked.

"A secret," Toni said. "And secrets change shape."

Zee nodded once. "They get heavier."

Jayda looked down at her hands again. For a moment, Toni thought she might push back, joke it away, say something about adults overreacting. Instead, Jayda let out a slow breath and said, "Okay."

Just that.

Okay.

It didn't sound like agreement so much as acceptance. Like stepping onto a scale and not looking away from the number.

Mikki felt something loosen in her chest. "We tell it together," she said. "All of it."

Zee added, "No fixing it on the way out of our mouths."

Jayda huffed a quiet laugh. "That's going to be hard."

"Yeah," Toni said. "That's how we'll know we're doing it right."

They didn't move right away.

The decision sat between them, solid now, no longer theoretical. Telling the truth wouldn't undo anything. It wouldn't rewind time or soften what had already landed. But it would change what came next.

And that mattered.

When they finally stood, they did it at the same time. No signal. No countdown.

Just four girls, choosing not to carry it alone.

They did not go inside right away.

The porch felt like a threshold, close enough to the house to count as safety, far enough from it to still breathe. The boards were warm under their feet, holding the day a little longer than the air wanted to. Cicadas buzzed unevenly now, louder than before, like they were trying to fill the space where no one was talking.

Jayda sat down first, dropping onto the top step with a soft thud. She rested her elbows on her knees and stared out at the yard. "I don't even know where to start," she said.

Mikki leaned against the porch post. "At the beginning."

Jayda scoffed lightly. "The *real* beginning or the version where we sound smarter."

"The real one," Zee said. "The one that makes your stomach hurt."

That earned a small, humorless smile from Jayda. "Cool. Love that for us."

Toni picked at a loose splinter on the step, then stopped herself. She could feel the words lining up in her head, already trying to shape the story into something cleaner. *This happened, then that happened, and here's why it makes sense.* She forced herself to let that go.

Truth doesn't need to be neat, she reminded herself.

"We should decide who says what," Mikki said. "So we don't talk over each other. Or leave things out by accident."

Jayda glanced up. "You mean on purpose."

Mikki didn't argue.

Zee uncrossed her arms and crouched, bringing herself closer to their eye level. "We each say our part," she said. "Not what we think it adds up to. Just what we did. What we noticed. What we ignored."

That landed differently.

Jayda rubbed her palms against her jeans. "Okay," she said slowly. "Then I'll say I kept going even after it felt easy. And that I didn't want to stop when it stopped feeling scary."

Mikki nodded. "I'll say I let efficiency replace checking. That I trusted the system because it had worked, not because I verified it again."

Zee swallowed. "I'll say I felt the shortcuts happening and didn't shut them down fast enough. That I assumed familiarity meant safety."

All three of them looked at Toni.

She hadn't realized she was holding her breath until she let it out. "I'll say I noticed things," she said. "And didn't always speak up because I wasn't sure I was right."

Jayda turned toward her. "You usually are."

"That doesn't count if I don't say it," Toni replied.

Silence settled again, but this time it felt steadier. Less sharp.

"So," Jayda said, pushing herself to her feet, "we're really doing this."

"Yes," Mikki said.

"Together," Zee added.

Jayda nodded once. "Okay."

The word sounded different now than it had before. Not resignation. Not fear.

Decision.

They didn't rehearse. They didn't polish their sentences. Whatever came out next would be rough by default, and that was the point.

When the screen door finally opened, the sound cut clean through the air.

Grandma Dot stood there, one hand on the frame, eyes moving calmly from face to face. She didn't ask why they were standing like that. She didn't rush them.

She just said, "Come on in," and stepped aside.

They followed her inside, carrying the truth with them.

Not as a weapon.

Not as a shield.

Just as it was.

They stood in the kitchen longer than necessary.

Not because anyone stopped them. Because stepping fully into the room felt like crossing another line, and lines had started to matter in new ways. The overhead light was too bright, flattening everything, leaving nowhere for shadows to hide. The table sat in the center like it always had, scarred and steady and familiar.

Grandma Dot took her place at the counter, not sitting yet. She wiped her hands once on a towel that didn't need it and looked at them again. Still no questions.

That made it harder.

Mikki felt the urge to fill the space rise up fast, the way it always did when silence stretched too long. Explanations wanted to rush out of her, already arranging themselves into order. Measurements. Logic. Sequence.

She stopped herself.

This wasn't about making sense yet.

Jayda went first, just like she had on the porch.

"We built something," she said. "And it worked. For a while."

Grandma Dot nodded. "Mm."

Zee shifted her weight. "We practiced. We tested. We followed rules. And then we bent them."

"How?," Grandma Dot asked, gently.

Mikki swallowed. "Small ways."

Jayda let out a breath. "The kind you don't notice right away."

Toni stared at the table, tracing one of the old scratches with her eyes. "The kind that don't feel dangerous because nothing bad happens at first."

That was when Grandma Dot sat down.

The chair scraped softly against the floor, grounding the moment. She folded her hands on the table and waited.

Jayda felt the words catch in her chest. "There was a moment today," she said, quieter now, "where something almost happened."

Grandma Dot didn't interrupt.

"The ladder moved," Mikki added. "Just a little. Enough that if someone hadn't been right there—"

"But nothing did happen," Jayda said quickly, then stopped. She pressed her lips together. "I know. That's not the point."

Grandma Dot looked at her. "Why isn't it?"

Jayda hesitated. "Because it means we were closer than we thought."

Zee nodded. "And because if it hadn't been today, it would've been another day. The conditions were lining up."

Toni finally looked up. "We realized we were starting to trust how it felt instead of checking how it was."

The kitchen went quiet.

Grandma Dot leaned back slightly, studying them. Not with anger. Not with disappointment.

With attention.

"Thank you for telling me," she said.

The words landed softly, but they carried weight.

Jayda blinked. "That's it."

"For now," Grandma Dot replied. "You didn't come in here to be punished. You came in here because you knew something mattered."

Mikki felt her shoulders loosen a fraction. "We wanted you to know before—"

"Before it turned into something you couldn't explain," Grandma Dot finished.

Zee let out a slow breath. "Yes."

Grandma Dot nodded again. "That's called responsibility."

The word didn't sting the way Jayda expected it to. It settled instead, heavy but solid.

"We're not asking to keep going," Toni said quickly. "I mean," Toni said, then steadied herself. "Not right now."

Grandma Dot smiled faintly. "I didn't think you were."

She stood and reached for the kettle, the familiar motion easing the room just enough. "The truth doesn't end a story," she said. "It tells you where you actually are."

Jayda glanced at the others, then back at her. "So... what happens next."

Grandma Dot turned back to them. "Now," she said, "we talk about what you learned."

And for the first time since the almost, no one felt the urge to rush ahead.

They did not tell Grandma Dot everything all at once.

It came in pieces, the way truth usually does when it matters.

First, Mikki spoke. She explained what they had built, how long it had taken, how carefully they had planned it. She talked about angles and checks and why she believed it was safe. She did not rush. She did not soften it. She did not excuse it either.

Zee filled in what Mikki left out. The knots. The rope. The way they reset and retested and then stopped resetting as often. She said it plainly, without dramatizing it, without protecting herself from how it sounded.

Toni talked last.

She explained what she noticed. Not as an accusation. Not as a list. Just observations. The way ready stopped being said. The way counting disappeared. The way normal arrived too quickly and stayed too long.

Jayda listened the whole time.

She did not interrupt. She did not joke. She did not shrug it off the way she usually did when conversations got uncomfortable. When it was her turn, she stared at the floor for a long moment before speaking.

"I didn't think I was being reckless," she said. "I thought I was being confident."

No one corrected her.

"That's why I didn't stop myself," she added. "Because nothing felt wrong."

The room stayed quiet after that.

Grandma Dot did not raise her voice. She did not ask who was at fault. She did not say you should have known better or I told you so. She did not reach for control the way adults sometimes did when fear disguised itself as authority.

Instead, she asked one question.

"When did you realize you needed to stop?"

The answer came faster than any of them expected.

"After," Mikki said.

"Almost," Zee said.

"When it stopped feeling scary," Jayda said.

Toni did not speak, but she nodded.

Grandma Dot absorbed that without reacting. She moved to the table and sat down, folding her hands together like she was making space for something heavier than rules.

"You are not in trouble for telling me," she said. "You would be in trouble for pretending nothing happened."

Jayda swallowed.

"This isn't about punishment," Grandma Dot continued. "It's about responsibility. And responsibility doesn't mean you never mess up. It means you do not hide when you realize you almost did."

No one argued with that.

"You made something," she said. "You learned something. And something almost went wrong."

Her gaze moved from face to face, not lingering too long on any one of them.

"So now," she said, "you tell me what you think should happen next."

The question landed differently than any lecture would have.

Mikki felt it settle in her chest. Zee straightened slightly. Toni's fingers tightened around her notebook. Jayda finally looked up.

They did not answer right away.

But they understood.

This part still belonged to them.

They decided together.

Not quickly. Not easily.

At first, the ideas came out tangled. Jayda suggested they just take it down forever. Zee pushed back, not because she wanted to keep running it, but because pretending it never existed felt wrong. Mikki worried out loud about whether stopping completely meant they had learned the right lesson or just retreated from it. Toni listened, absorbing everything, turning it over in her mind like she always did.

Grandma Dot stayed quiet.

That was deliberate.

Eventually, the shape of it began to settle.

"We don't run it again," Jayda said finally. "Not like before."

Zee nodded. "And if we touch it at all, it's not to test it. It's to understand what changed."

Mikki added, "And we write everything down again. Every check. Every step. Even if it feels repetitive."

Toni looked up. "Especially if it feels repetitive."

That earned a small smile from Zee.

They sat with that for a moment, making sure it felt real and not performative. Making sure it wasn't just words meant to sound responsible.

"And," Jayda said quietly, "if any one of us says stop, we stop. No arguing."

No one hesitated.

"That part is non negotiable," Mikki said.

Grandma Dot nodded once. "That sounds like boundaries," she said. "Not fear."

She stood then, signaling the end of the conversation without cutting it off too sharply. "You'll show me what you're doing next time. Not because I don't trust you. Because trust doesn't mean absence."

That mattered.

Jayda exhaled slowly. "Thank you."

"For telling the truth," Grandma Dot replied. "Not for being perfect."

After she left the room, the four of them stayed where they were.

The silence felt different now. Not heavy. Not sharp. More like the quiet after something fragile had been set down carefully instead of dropped.

Toni opened her notebook at last.

She did not write diagrams or measurements. She wrote one sentence, slow and deliberate, then closed the book again.

We are responsible for what we build, and for when we stop.

Jayda leaned back in her chair. "I don't like how grown that sounded."

Zee snorted. "Too late."

Mikki didn't smile, but something in her shoulders finally loosened.

They had not fixed everything.

But they had done the part that mattered most.

They had told the truth before it was forced out of them.

And that changed what came next.

Chapter 17
Learning to Hold Again

The yard looked wider without the rope.

Not emptier. Just stretched, like a breath held a little longer than usual. The space between The Lookout and The Launch Tree was clean and open, nothing pulled tight between them, nothing humming or waiting. The grass beneath where the line used to run had begun to lift again, blades slowly untangling themselves from the memory of weight. In places, it leaned a little differently, as if it had been pressed down for long enough to remember, but not long enough to stay that way.

Jayda noticed that first.

She stayed near the edge of the yard, her weight shifted carefully to one side, the cast at her leg a solid presence she could not ignore. One crutch rested under her arm, the other leaned against the porch rail within easy reach. Her hands hung loose at her sides as her eyes traced the invisible path out of habit, following it without her body needing to move. Her muscles still remembered where the start had been. Where the drop came. Where she always began to slow.

That knowledge lived in her muscles, quiet but persistent.

The absence tugged at her anyway, a soft pull that didn't ask permission and didn't demand to be followed. It simply existed, like a memory that hadn't decided whether it was finished yet.

She didn't step forward.

She didn't test how close she could get.

The cast made that choice easier, in a way. It enforced distance without asking her to explain it.

Zee knelt near the fence where the rope had been coiled the day before. The coil was gone now, stored away where it couldn't be reached without choosing to reach for it. She rested her palms on the grass instead, fingers splayed, grounding herself in the cool, damp feel of it. The earth didn't rush her. It didn't argue. It stayed where it was, steady and patient.

That mattered.

Mikki stayed back by the porch, arms folded loosely, gaze steady but softer than it had been before. She wasn't measuring anything. Not angles. Not distance. Not the gap between where things had gone wrong and where they stood now. She let the yard exist without turning it into numbers, and the restraint felt heavier than any calculation she'd ever carried.

Toni stood between them, notebook tucked under her arm like it had been for days now. She didn't open it. She didn't need to. The yard didn't require recording yet.

This part was for noticing.

The cicadas buzzed from the trees, steady and insistent, though not as loud as they had been earlier in the summer. The sound felt thinner now, like it was already beginning to let go. A breeze moved through the branches overhead, sending shadows sliding across the grass where the rope once cut a clean line through the air.

Jayda watched the shadows pass and felt something loosen in her chest.

Not relief exactly.

More like space.

No one said, *We're not rebuilding today.*

They didn't have to.

The absence said it for them.

It sat between the trees and along the porch boards, quiet but unmistakable. Not a rule yet. Not an agreement. Just a fact that no one felt the need to challenge. The yard did not invite them forward. It did not push them away either. It simply existed, unchanged and uninterested in their decision.

A breeze moved through the trees again, slower this time, stirring leaves overhead and sending another ripple of shadow across the grass where the rope once cut a clean line through the air. The motion was familiar enough that Jayda tracked it automatically, her eyes following the path the shadow made as it slid and disappeared.

She felt something ease in her chest as it passed.

Not relief exactly.

More like permission.

"We're really not touching it," she said finally.

Her voice didn't sound unsure. It didn't sound brave either. It sounded like she was checking a door before closing it, making sure everyone else was on the same side.

Zee shook her head once. "Not yet."

Mikki nodded. "Not today."

The words settled without argument.

Jayda exhaled, slow and deliberate, the way she had learned to do when her body felt tighter than the moment called for. "Okay."

The word didn't feel like giving something up. It didn't land with disappointment or loss. It felt like setting something down carefully, palms open, knowing exactly where it was and choosing not to carry it for a while.

They stayed where they were.

No one drifted closer to the trees. No one stepped off the porch without meaning to. The yard remained just a yard again. No system. No test. No proof required.

Toni noticed that before she noticed anything else.

She shifted her weight slightly, then stilled herself, aware of how quiet the group had become. Not tense. Not frozen. Just attentive in a way that didn't demand action. Her notebook pressed lightly against her side, familiar and present, but she didn't reach for it.

She thought, *this is what holding looks like.*

The thought surprised her. It didn't arrive dressed up or polished. It came plain and steady, like something that didn't need to be examined yet to be understood.

She didn't write it down.

Not yet.

A lawn mower started somewhere down the block, the sound rising and falling as it moved along someone else's yard. The noise felt far away, like the world continuing at a respectful distance. Somewhere nearby, a door opened and closed. Voices drifted faintly and then disappeared.

Jayda shifted her weight carefully, adjusting where she stood so the cast didn't pull. The movement was small, but it reminded her how much her body was still doing even when she wasn't. Healing didn't announce itself. It worked quietly, asking for patience more than effort.

"We don't have to decide anything else today," Mikki said, not as a suggestion but as a boundary she was setting for herself as much as anyone else.

Zee glanced at her, then back at the yard. "That feels right."

Jayda nodded once. "Today can just be this."

The word *this* didn't need explaining.

They let it be enough.

The cicadas surged again, louder for a moment, then softened, the sound thinning as if the afternoon itself was starting to tire. The shadows stretched longer across the porch boards, edges blurring where sunlight had been sharp earlier.

No one moved to interrupt it.

They were learning, without saying so, that stopping didn't always mean ending. Sometimes it meant staying exactly where you were until the moment passed on its own.

And for now, that was the only choice any of them needed to make.

They did not return to their old places.

That was the first change anyone noticed once the decision not to rebuild settled into something solid.

Before, they would have spread out without thinking. Someone on the grass. Someone leaning against the tree. Someone pacing the distance like movement itself was part of the plan. Now, the porch drew them in instead, its edges defined and familiar, offering limits without making them feel trapped.

Jayda shifted carefully and lowered herself onto the porch steps. It took a moment to find the right angle, one where the cast didn't pull and the pressure along her leg stayed manageable. She adjusted once, then again, until the position stopped asking so much of her. One crutch rested against the railing beside her, close enough to grab without thinking. The other lay flat along the step, its rubber tip pressed firmly into the wood.

She hated how deliberate everything felt now.
She also knew it was necessary.

Zee leaned against the porch post, one shoulder pressed into the painted wood. She kept her feet planted, toes angled outward, grounding herself through contact instead of motion. From here, she could see the yard clearly without being drawn into it. That felt important.

Mikki took the edge of the bench, not centered, not in charge. She sat the way you do when you're trying not to claim too much space, hands resting loosely on her knees, posture alert but restrained. It took effort not to straighten the bench, not to check whether it was level, not to count the boards beneath her feet.

She didn't do any of that.

Toni remained standing a moment longer than the rest. She stayed near the doorway, notebook tucked under her arm, watching the way the group arranged itself without being told to. The shifts were subtle. The distance between them measured differently now. Not farther apart. Just intentional.

When she finally sat, it was close enough to hear everyone breathe.

No one had assigned seats.

They had simply chosen distance differently.

The porch creaked softly as the weight settled. The sound felt louder than usual, as if the house itself was paying attention.

"We can't pretend it didn't happen," Mikki said finally.

She didn't look at anyone in particular when she said it. Her gaze stayed somewhere between the yard and the porch boards, steady and fixed, like she was speaking to the space as much as the people in it. Her voice was quieter than usual, but it didn't waver.

"But we also can't act like it means we're done forever."

The words hung there, not demanding agreement but waiting for it.

Jayda nodded slowly. The movement tugged slightly at her neck, a reminder that even small gestures carried weight now. "I don't want to be done," she said. Her voice was even, but her hands tightened briefly in the pockets of her hoodie. "I just don't want to rush back into it like nothing changed."

Zee crossed her arms, then uncrossed them again, the motion restless before she caught herself and stilled her hands against the post. "We need rules," she said. "Different ones."

"Stricter," Mikki added without hesitation.

Jayda made a face. "I knew you were going to say that."

The corner of Mikki's mouth twitched, but she didn't argue.

"Clearer," Toni said, surprising herself by speaking up. The word felt heavier once it was out in the open. "So we don't argue about what we meant later."

That landed.

Mikki turned then and really looked at her. Not the way you glance at someone while already thinking ahead. The way you look when you're willing to let what they said change something. She nodded once. "Yes," she said. "Clear."

The word settled between them, simple and firm.

Clear.

The cicadas buzzed in the background, steady and loud enough to fill the spaces where no one rushed to speak again. The porch held. The yard stayed quiet.

They sat with the shape of what they were becoming, aware that where they placed themselves now mattered as much as anything they said next.

They let the word sit between them.

Clear.

It sounded simple when you said it out loud. Cleaner than stricter. Kinder than control. But it carried weight, the kind that didn't move unless you acknowledged it.

The cicadas buzzed in the background, steady and loud enough to fill the spaces where no one rushed to speak. The porch held the sound without echoing it back. The yard stayed quiet, unchanged, as if it were listening without comment.

Zee was the first to break the stillness.

"Rule one," she said.

She didn't raise her voice. She didn't shift her stance. She just spoke, the words landing flat and even, like she was placing something down instead of throwing it into the middle.

"We don't rebuild anything without all four of us there. Not watching. Not nearby. There."

Jayda lifted her hand slightly, the movement small but deliberate. "Agreed."

It mattered that she said it out loud. Toni felt that. Agreement spoken had a different shape than agreement assumed.

Mikki nodded once. She didn't add anything yet. She was waiting to see if the rule held on its own.

It did.

"Rule two," Mikki said then. "If someone says stop, we stop. No explaining first. No finishing the run."

Toni felt the words press into her chest before she realized why. Explaining had always felt harmless before. Reasonable. Something you did to smooth things over. Hearing it named as something to pause made her understand how easily momentum disguised itself as logic.

"No convincing," she said quietly.

Zee glanced at her, then nodded. "Especially no convincing."

Jayda swallowed. Her eyes flicked toward the yard and back again. "Okay."

She said it like she meant it, even though it cost her something.

"Rule three," Mikki continued. "We check everything every time. Even if it feels boring. Even if it feels unnecessary."

Jayda let out a breath and tilted her head back against the porch rail. "I hate that one."

Zee didn't smile. "That's how we know it's important."

A corner of Jayda's mouth lifted anyway. "Fair."

They paused after that, the quiet stretching without pressure. Toni was aware of her notebook again, the way it pressed against her side like it wanted to be opened. She resisted the urge. Writing too soon would flatten this into something finished before it was ready.

"There's one more," she said instead.

All three of them turned toward her.

The attention felt heavier than she expected, but it didn't make her retreat.

"If someone feels off," Toni continued, choosing her words slowly, "even if they can't explain why, that counts too."

Mikki's shoulders eased just slightly, the tension she'd been holding loosening in a way that was almost invisible. "Yes," she said. "That counts."

Zee nodded. "That might be the most important one."

Jayda stared out at the yard, her gaze tracing the empty space between the trees before returning to them. "So we're not just rebuilding a thing," she said. "We're rebuilding how we do it."

"Exactly," Mikki said.

Jayda let out a breath she hadn't realized she'd been holding. It moved through her slowly, like she was making room for something new. "Okay," she said. "I can do that."

No one cheered.

No one clapped.

The rules didn't need noise to make them real.

They sat with them, letting the shape of what they had named settle into the space around them. The cicadas kept buzzing. The porch stayed steady beneath them. The yard remained untouched.

For the first time since the fall, the agreement felt less like something they were trying to prevent and more like something they were choosing to build.

They did not go near the trees.

That was intentional.

Instead, they stayed where they were, on the porch and along the edges of the yard, close enough to see the space clearly but far enough away that it remained untouched. The absence felt loud at first, like a missing note in a song they all knew too well. It hummed at the edge of their awareness, asking to be filled.

Jayda felt it most.

Her eyes kept drifting toward the gap between The Lookout and The Launch Tree, tracking the distance the way she always had, instinctively mapping where motion would begin and end. Each time she noticed herself doing it, she stopped. Not sharply.

Not with frustration. Just enough to interrupt the habit before it carried her somewhere she was not ready to go.

Zee noticed.

Mikki noticed too.

No one commented.

Zee disappeared briefly into the house and came back with the rope, still coiled tight. She set it down on the porch steps instead of the grass, placing it carefully, like it might change shape if she rushed. The fibers looked the same as they always had, rough and familiar, but the way she handled them had slowed.

"We're not testing tension," Zee said. "We're checking condition."

Jayda leaned forward slightly, careful not to shift her weight too far. The cast limited how close she could get, and she let it. "So we're... looking."

"Looking," Zee agreed.

She ran her fingers along the rope, slow and deliberate, pausing where the fibers felt uneven, where wear had begun to hide inside familiarity. She did not pull. She did not lift. She just read it the way she always had, hands translating information her eyes could not catch on their own.

Mikki watched from the bench, hands folded loosely in her lap. She resisted the urge to count. Not because the numbers weren't there, but because she wanted to see what happened when she didn't reach for them right away. Instead, she paid attention to the order of things. Zee's pauses. Jayda's stillness. The way Toni's gaze moved back and forth between them, tracking without recording.

Toni opened her notebook just long enough to write one line in the margin.

What we check when we don't ride.

She closed it again before the page filled up. One line was enough for now.

They practiced saying stop.

Zee said it first, lifting her hand, palm open.

Jayda froze where she sat, attention snapping into place as a sharp twinge shot through her leg. It faded quickly, but it left a warning behind, clear and unmistakable. Her body responded even though it didn't move, muscles tightening in a way that felt both familiar and new. Stopping without momentum felt strange. Like slamming on brakes that hadn't been engaged.

"Again," Zee said.

Toni said it next. The word came out softer than Zee's, but it still landed. Jayda felt it settle in her chest, the pause stretching just long enough to be felt.

"Again," Mikki said.

This time the word carried weight, not because it was louder, but because it was chosen. Jayda nodded once, acknowledging it without needing anything else to follow.

Each repetition made the word clearer. Less reactive. More deliberate.

"That matters," Mikki said.

Jayda nodded. "It feels weird."

"It should," Mikki replied. "That means it's interrupting momentum."

They let that sit.

Zee moved on to the harness next, lifting it carefully and setting it beside the rope. She adjusted one strap, then another, narrating quietly as she went so no step disappeared into habit.

"Clip check. Strap alignment. Wear points," she said. "Same order every time."

Jayda repeated the list under her breath, not mocking, not joking. Just learning it the way you learn something you plan to keep.

Toni watched the repetition settle into rhythm. Practice without motion. Attention without speed. It felt incomplete and that was the point.

When they finished, no one reached for the trees.

No one suggested trying just one run.

They stayed where they were, letting the rules exist without testing them yet.

That was different too.

They stayed where they were.

Close, but not crowded. The rope lay coiled on the porch steps beside them, not in the way, not forgotten either. The yard remained open and empty, the space between The Lookout and The Launch Tree untouched, as if it had agreed to wait.

Jayda broke the quiet first.

"I don't miss the flying part right now," she said. Her voice surprised her with how steady it sounded. "I miss knowing exactly what we're doing."

Mikki nodded. "That comes back."

Zee added, "Only if we build it."

The words didn't feel like a warning. They felt like a condition.

Toni watched the light shift across the porch boards, the way the grain caught the sun and then let it go again. Something settled where panic had been earlier.

Not confidence.

Not fear.

Attention.

She opened her notebook and wrote one last line, slow enough that the words did not rush each other.

Holding starts before you ever let go.

She closed the notebook and rested her hand on the cover, feeling the solidness of it beneath her palm.

They stayed until the sun softened, light sliding from gold into something gentler, less demanding. Grandma Dot came out once with a pitcher of lemonade and glasses that clinked softly when she set them down. She did not ask questions. She did not offer instructions. She left the pitcher between them and went back inside.

That felt like trust.

Jayda poured the drinks, careful with her movements, handing the first glass to Toni without thinking. Toni took it without comment. Zee took hers next. Mikki waited, watching the way Jayda adjusted, noticing without stepping in.

Nothing was fixed.

Not completely.

Jayda still flinched when a branch snapped in the distance. Mikki still replayed moments she wished she could rewind. Zee still woke some mornings with her hands clenched like they were holding invisible rope. Toni still felt the pull to write everything down before it could change shape.

But the quiet no longer felt fragile.

They sat on the porch steps as the evening settled in around them, the cicadas rising and falling like breath. No one reached for the rope. No one suggested moving closer to the trees. The choice not to touch it stayed firm without being announced.

They learned, in that stillness, that restraint could hold just as much weight as action.

When they finally stood to go inside, Jayda moved carefully, crutches steady beneath her hands. No one rushed her. No one pretended not to notice.

They went in together.

The yard stayed behind them, open and ordinary again. The space between the trees remained empty, and for once, that emptiness did not feel like a problem to solve.

It felt like something they had learned to live with.

And for now, that was enough.

Chapter 18
The Shape of the Story

Toni sat alone at the small desk by the window, her notebook open but untouched. The page was blank, not because she did not know what to write, but because she knew too many wrong ways to begin.

She flipped backward instead.

Early pages rustled softly under her fingers. Diagrams. Half sentences Urgent notes written like if she did not catch the moment fast enough, it would disappear. She recognized the handwriting immediately. The pressure. The speed. The need.

She had wanted the story to hurry then.

Back when flying still felt like the most important part.

Toni paused on a page filled almost edge to edge, arrows pointing everywhere, margins crowded with thoughts stacked on top of each other. It looked breathless now. Like it was trying to prove something.

She closed the notebook gently.

The story was not about the fall.

That part was loud, but it was not the center.

It was not about bravery either, or recklessness, or how close they came to something worse. Those were the parts people leaned toward when they heard what happened, the sharp edges that made it easier to react.

Toni knew better now.

Those moments were real, but they were not the shape. They were just pressure points, places where the story bent.

She stared out the window at the yard, empty and ordinary, the trees standing the same way they always had. Nothing about them explained what had happened. Nothing about them apologized either.

The story did not owe anyone drama.
It did not owe anyone a lesson.

It only owed the truth, told carefully.

Toni picked up her pen, then set it down again. Not yet. She needed to understand the outline first, the negative space around the words.

Some stories were not meant to rush toward an ending. Some needed to be held still long enough to see what they were not.

She let the notebook stay open on the desk, blank page waiting, patient in a way she was finally learning to be.

Toni wrote slowly this time.

Not full sentences at first. Just words. Shapes of ideas she could move around without committing to them yet. She let the pen rest between thoughts, gave herself permission to pause.

The story felt wider than she had expected.

It stretched backward into the days before the zipline, before the idea had taken hold, before flying had seemed like something they could touch. It stretched forward too, past the fall, past the apologies and the quiet days that followed, into a place she could not see clearly yet but knew existed.

That mattered.

Stories were not straight lines. She knew that now. They curved. They folded back on themselves. Sometimes they revealed their meaning only after you had walked past it.

She flipped forward again, stopping near the end of the notebook where the pages were still crisp and untouched. The blankness no longer felt like pressure. It felt like space.

Toni wrote one sentence, then stopped.

She read it once. Then again.

It did not explain everything. It was not dramatic. It did not sound impressive. But it was true.

She left it there.

Outside, the afternoon light shifted, slower than it used to feel. The sun caught the edge of the window and warmed the desk beneath her hands. She noticed it without rushing to name it.

That was new too.

Toni thought about the others.

About Mikki, who would probably always count first and feel later, even as she learned that numbers could not carry everything. About Zee, whose hands remembered responsibility long after the danger had passed. About Jayda, whose confidence had cracked just enough to let something steadier grow in its place.

None of them were the same.

That did not mean they were broken.

The shape of the story was not the moment they fell.

It was the way they learned where the ground actually was.

Toni added another line beneath the first, smaller this time. She did not underline it. She did not circle it. She trusted herself to find it again.

For the first time since the beginning, she did not feel like she was chasing the story.

She was listening to it.

Toni closed the notebook.

Not because she was finished. Because she knew where to stop.

Some things wanted to be written down so they could be carried. Others wanted to stay loose, held in the body instead of the page. She was learning the difference.

She rested the notebook against her chest for a moment, feeling the quiet weight of it there. The room around her breathed the way it always had. The faint hum of the house. The muted sounds of life continuing in small, ordinary ways.

She thought about what she would not write.

She would not write the sound of the rope snapping. She would not write the way fear had sharpened everything that day, or how close it had come to stealing something from them they could not have gotten back. Those memories already lived where they needed to live.

What she would write instead were the choices.

The way they stopped. The way they told the truth. The way no one tried to pretend it had been nothing. The way they learned to hold each other without holding too tight.

That was the shape she wanted to keep.

Toni stood and slid the notebook onto the shelf beside the others, not at the end, not hidden, just placed where it belonged. She stepped back and looked at it for a second longer than necessary.

The story did not feel finished.

But it felt whole enough to rest.

Outside, the light softened again, evening moving in without asking permission. Toni let it. She did not rush to capture it. Some moments were allowed to pass without becoming proof.

She turned away from the shelf and went to find the others.

The story would continue.

She did not need to force it.

She knew now that it already knew how to move

Chapter 19
We Are Back in The World

School smelled like pencil shavings and cafeteria pizza again.

The halls were loud in the way they always were between classes, lockers slamming, voices overlapping, sneakers squeaking against the floor. It felt strange how normal everything looked, how easily the world had moved on.

Jayda moved carefully through the hallway, her crutches clicking in a steady rhythm against the floor. The cast on her leg was white and bulky, already marked with ink. Someone had drawn a crooked star near the ankle. Someone else had written *feel better* in bubble letters. She pretended not to mind.

Zee walked beside her without hovering. Mikki stayed a step ahead, already clearing a path through the crowd. Toni followed just behind, notebook tucked under her arm, eyes tracking everything the way they always did.

"That nickname is not sticking," Jayda said.

Zee didn't look over. "It already has."

Jayda sighed. "Unbelievable."

Malik stopped in front of them like he had been waiting for the timing to feel right.

He took in the crutches first. Then the cast. Then her face. His mouth tilted into a grin.

"So," he said. "I hear they calling you Crash Queen now."

Jayda closed her eyes. "Please keep walking."

Malik ignored that. "I told you something was gonna happen. I distinctly remember warning y'all."

"You distinctly remember running your mouth," Zee said.

Malik nodded. "Details."

Andre lingered a few steps back, pretending not to watch while clearly watching.

Malik tilted his head. "So what happened? You try to fly for real."

Jayda opened one eye. "I did not fly."

"Fall," Malik corrected. "With commitment."

Mikki crossed her arms. "It was a controlled descent."

Malik blinked. "That is exactly what I mean."

Jayda laughed before she could stop herself. It surprised her how easy it felt.

Malik's grin softened just a little. "You good though? For real?"

Jayda nodded. "Yeah. I will be."

He nodded back, then pointed at the cast. "So. Can I sign it?"

She raised an eyebrow. "You just spent thirty seconds saying you told me so."

"History matters," Malik said. "I wanna be on the record."

Jayda shifted her weight and held the cast out. "Fine. But don't draw anything stupid."

Malik pulled a marker from his pocket like he had been waiting all morning. He bent carefully, tongue caught between his teeth, and wrote his name in neat block letters along the side.

He added a small crown over the C in Crash.

"There," he said, straightening. "Official."

Jayda looked at it, then at him. "You're annoying."

"True," Malik said. "But memorable."

The bell rang, sharp and sudden.

Malik backed away, hands up. "Heal up, Crash Queen."

Jayda smiled, slow and real this time. "Mind your business."

He laughed and disappeared into the crowd.

Jayda adjusted her backpack and moved forward again, crutches tapping a little louder now in the rush of bodies. Zee stayed close without saying anything. Mikki glanced back once to check spacing. Toni waited until the hall thinned before following.

They turned the corner together.

The math classroom door stood open, sunlight slanting across the floor. Jayda stepped inside last and stopped.

She looked up.

Zee was already sliding into a desk near the window. Mikki took a seat two rows over, bag placed neatly beneath the chair. Toni settled between them, notebook out before the room fully quieted.

All four of them.

Same class. Same room.

Jayda let out a breath she hadn't realized she was holding and maneuvered carefully into her seat, stretching the cast forward so it wouldn't catch on the desk.

The board at the front of the room was already filled with numbers. Angles. Lines waiting to be measured.

The teacher cleared her throat.

Jayda glanced sideways at the others.

They were ready.

Not to run.

Not to fly.

Just to notice.

The bell rang again, and class began.

Epilogue
How We Flew That Summer

They would talk about that summer later like it had been loud. Like it had been full of motion and shouting and the kind of stories that get told with hands waving in the air. People liked to imagine flying as something dramatic, something you could point to and say, *there*, that was it.

But that was not how it felt to Toni when she thought back on it.

Flying, as it turned out, had been small.

It had been early mornings that did not rush them. It had been the way the yard looked before anything was built, and the way it looked again after everything was taken down. It had been the space between decisions, the pauses that mattered more than the jumps.

Back then, she had thought flying meant speed. Height. The moment when your feet left the ground and your stomach followed a split second later. She had believed it was something you did with your body first and understood afterward, if at all.

Now she knew better.

What stayed with her was not the movement, but the awareness. The way time had stretched around them that summer, wide enough to notice details they usually missed. The way silence had taught them things noise never could. The way stopping had felt harder than going, and therefore more important.

They had not flown because the zipline worked.

They had flown because they learned when not to use it.

That summer did not sparkle in her memory. It did not replay like a highlight reel. It rested instead, steady and quiet, like something solid you could lean on without fear of it giving way.

When Toni thought of flying now, she did not picture the air. She pictured the ground.

And how carefully, deliberately, they learned where it was.

They learned it together, not all at once.

Mikki learned it first in numbers that finally admitted their limits. She still counted. She always would. But she stopped pretending that counting meant control. She learned to leave room in her plans for the parts that could not be measured, the parts that lived in people instead of systems. She learned that responsibility was not proven by being right, but by being willing to stop.

Zee learned it in her hands. In the way she slowed them down on purpose, even when muscle memory begged her to move faster. She learned that strength was not just about holding things steady, but about knowing when to let go before something tightened too far. She learned that care could be quiet and still be firm.

Jayda learned it in the space where her confidence cracked and did not shatter. She learned that courage did not disappear when fear showed up. It changed shape. It became listening. It became asking instead of assuming. It became choosing steadiness over speed, even when speed had always loved her back.

And Toni learned it in the writing.

She learned that stories were not trophies you earned by surviving something dramatic. They were containers. They held what you noticed, what you chose, what you refused to rush past. She learned that some truths arrived loud and others arrived slowly, and both deserved to be treated with care.

They did not stop being themselves that summer.

They became more precise versions of who they already were.

Flying had not lifted them away from the ground. It had taught them how to stand on it together without pretending they were alone.

They did not rebuild the zipline.

That choice surprised people later, the ones who heard the story in pieces and expected a different ending. They expected a return. A redo. A cleaner version where the fear was gone and the fun came back louder than before.

But summer taught them that endings did not always need replacements.

The yard stayed open. Ordinary. The space between The Lookout and The Launch Tree filled with other things instead. Long talks that stretched past sunset. Cards spread across the porch floor. Quiet afternoons where no one needed to prove anything. They learned the shape of the place without trying to pull tension through it.

Sometimes Jayda still ran the distance, arms wide, stopping herself just short of where the landing hay used to be. She laughed when she did it, breathless and bright, then let herself slow down on purpose.

Mikki watched the wind more than the rope that was no longer there. She noticed how it shifted, how it changed its mind, how it refused to be predicted. She stopped seeing that as a problem.

Zee fixed other things. A loose step. A bent hinge. A fence panel that leaned too far to the left. She worked carefully, checking twice, stopping when her hands told her to. Nothing urgent. Nothing rushed.

Toni wrote less, but noticed more. She carried the story differently now, letting it live alongside them instead of ahead of them. When she did write, it was with space around the words, room for breath.

They flew that summer.

Not because they left the ground.

Because they learned when not to.

They learned the sound of balance.

It was not loud. It did not announce itself the way the snap of a rope did or the rush of air rushing past your ears. Balance sounded like mornings that started slow and stayed that way. Like footsteps moving through the house without urgency. Like laughter that rose and fell without tipping into something sharp.

They went back to the woods eventually. Not to build. To walk. To notice how the ground dipped in places they had ignored before. How branches bent under weight and then returned to themselves. How nothing stayed still for long, and how that was not a failure.

Jayda learned how to pause mid-motion. She still moved fast, still loved momentum, but now she stopped on purpose sometimes, just to feel where her body was before deciding where it should go next.

Mikki stopped believing that certainty was the same thing as safety. She still counted. She always would. But she let herself sit with answers that did not resolve cleanly, and she learned that some problems were meant to be watched, not solved.

Zee learned that being careful did not mean being afraid. It meant being present. She trusted her hands again, not because nothing could go wrong, but because she knew what to do when it did.

And Toni learned that stories did not belong to the loudest moment. They belonged to the quiet decisions that followed, the ones no one applauded but everyone lived inside.

That was how the summer held them.

Not as heroes.

Not as victims.

Just as four girls who learned how to move through the air of their own lives without needing to leave the ground.

They did not talk about the zipline much after that.

Not because it was forbidden. Not because it hurt too much. It just stopped being the center of things. It became a reference point instead of a destination, something they carried quietly the way you carry a scar you do not need to explain.

Summer kept happening.

There were evenings on the porch with legs tangled together, cicadas loud enough to drown out everything else. There were half-finished projects abandoned in the grass. There were days that stretched too long and others that vanished before anyone was ready. Life moved the way it always had, uneven and ordinary.

Sometimes Jayda would look up at the trees and grin, like she was remembering something private. Sometimes Mikki would pause mid-sentence, recalculating not numbers but tone. Sometimes Zee would tighten a knot that did not need tightening, then relax her hands and laugh at herself. Sometimes Toni would write for pages and sometimes not at all.

They learned that flying was never about leaving the ground.

It was about trust.

About timing.

About knowing when to hold on and when to let go.

It was about understanding that movement did not have to mean escape, and that stopping did not have to mean failure.

They had flown that summer.

Not because they built something daring.

Not because they fell.

But because they learned how to carry themselves through fear, through choice, through consequence, and still come out holding one another steady.

When the season finally shifted and the air cooled, the woods looked the same as they always had. Trees standing. Ground solid beneath their feet. Nothing marking the exact place where everything had changed.

That felt right.

Some stories did not need a monument.

Some only needed to be remembered correctly.

And they remembered this one the way it deserved to be remembered.

Together.

Toni's Notebook

Dear Diary,

Maybe we gave up too soon.

Not in a reckless way. Not like before. But maybe we stopped when we only needed to pause.

I keep thinking about how quiet the yard felt after everything. Not empty. Just waiting. Like it knew we were done for now, not forever.

Next summer does not have to look like last summer.

What if we build something that stays close to the ground. What if nothing leaves the porch. What if it is about balance instead of speed.

A bridge made of boards we test twice. A swing that never goes higher than we can reach. A system that teaches instead of dares.

Something you can stop halfway and still call finished.

I think that is the part we did not know before. That stopping does not mean failing. It means choosing the right ending.

Jayda says she does not miss flying the way she thought she would. She misses knowing.

Zee still checks knots in her sleep.

Mikki counts everything, but she listens now too.

And me. I am learning that writing things down is not the same as deciding them.

So maybe this is not the end of the story. Maybe it is the page where we leave space.

Next summer is a long way away. That feels okay.

Some things are better when you let them wait.

About The Author

Christina Jenkins writes stories shaped by attention, responsibility, and the quiet moments that change how people move through the world. A graduate of Clark Atlanta University and Mercer University, she has spent years working as an elementary school math and science teacher, listening closely to how children think, notice patterns, test boundaries, and learn where trust begins.

Her writing grows out of lived observation and a belief that meaning is often found in what happens between big moments. She is especially drawn to stories that center Black girls as thinkers, builders, and witnesses, not as symbols, but as fully present participants in their own lives.

Christina's work explores how systems are learned, how confidence forms, and how accountability takes shape long before it is named. She writes with care for the ways young people carry responsibility, experiment with independence, and learn to hold one another through change.

Her faith informs her understanding of stewardship, truth, and endurance. Through her storytelling, she seeks to honor the everyday acts that shape character and to remind readers that growth often begins in moments that feel small, ordinary, and unfinished.